THE SECRET (̣ ̱ ̱

Volume I of IV

by

Edwin A. Radcliffe

A Casdec Book

THE SECRET OF LIFE
Volume I of IV

First Published November 1995

Published by
Casdec Ltd
22 Harraton Terrace
Birtley
Chester-le-Street
Co Durham
DH3 2QG

Telephone 0191 410 5556
Fax 0191 410 0229

ISBN 0 907595 96 0

DEDICATION

To the strongest person I have known in this life, my own mother,
'Little Jenny'. Four feet ten inches of sheer grit, determination, love
and spiritual strength.

Truly a gigantic soul in so tiny a body.
Through her came so much of the truth.

Yours Truly
April 1995

FOREWORD

The four volumes of this book hold a true account of some of the incidents which have occurred in my life between 1973 and 1995.

It all began with the visit of a spirit entity in 1973 and the subsequent hundreds of visits and contacts since that time.

I was then thirty eight years old and contented with my very modest and established life pattern.

In no way did I have any prior interest in the events which started with that first visitation, nor did I have any prior knowledge of all that was to be revealed. I even supposed at one point that the entity was an alien, materialising by means of very advanced science.

The book tells of the purpose of the visits and of the gift of spiritual healing which came with them. Also of the teachings brought by the spirit guides.

All this had a profound effect upon the lives of many people around me, some amusing incidents, some emotional and some absolute miracles.

I have attempted to pass on many of the lessons which I have been taught by the guides, within the limitations of my intellect. In these lessons is contained 'The Secret of Life'.

The truth does not belong solely to Churches and religious sects and cannot be influenced by dogma, creed or fanaticism. Herein is the truth and those who are ready will recognise it.

Edwin A. Radcliffe.

Volume I Contents

Volume II Contents

Volume III Contents

Volume IV Contents

Chapter 1

Another Life Form
Westgate-on-Sea June 1973

Another Life Form

9 *suppose it all began in   June 1973 whilst I was on holiday at Westgate-on-Sea near Margate. I was then thirty eight years old and had been married for sixteen years to Beryl. We have two children, Sonja and Dale. Sonja was then ten years old and Dale was nearly three. This was a good time in our lives, we had worked hard and owned a nice little house and a car and I certainly felt that we had achieved our main goals and that there was the whole of life before us to be enjoyed.*

My father had passed away eighteen months earlier and so we took my mother on holiday with us.

At the time, I was working as a draughtsman at a small engineering firm in Sheffield.

The hotel we were staying in was right on the sea front and we had a room at the back which looked out over a field in those days. My mother was given a small room across the corridor from us. In our room we had a double bed to the left of the door and a bunk bed for Sonja and Dale across the room and to the right of the window. I seem to remember that it was a good sized room so we had plenty of space. We had travelled down on Saturday and although it was only two hundred miles from Sheffield we were all pretty tired that first night as the traffic had been quite bad.

About three o' clock in the morning I was woken by the sounds of my daughter, Sonja, struggling and grunting, it sounded as if she was trying to get out of bed in the darkness. Raising up I peered across the room but couldn't see a thing as there were no lights to the rear of the hotel. I remembered that there was a small reading lamp on the little cupboard at my side of the bed and after a few attempts, managed to switch it on. Sonja was hanging off the rail on the top deck of the bunk bed with her back to the bed and her feet waving about trying to stand on something solid. She was almost kicking Dale's face as he slept peacefully through all this in the lower bed. As the light went on, Sonja started to pull herself back up and before I could get across the room to her, was safely back on the top deck. She had missed the ladder by eighteen inches. I reached the bunk bed and as my wife and Dale were still sound asleep I whispered to Sonja, "What is the matter? Do you want to go to the toilet?" By this time she had covered herself up and did not answer. I realised that she was in fact, still asleep. In a louder whisper, I repeated the question, but she just slept on. All this I found a little worrying for I realised that she had been involved in a form of sleep-walking, which I had never known her to do before. I put this down to the tiring journey and went back to bed to sleep soundly until morning with no further disturbances.

We had a perfect Sunday on the beach, the weather was good and we were all in high spirits by evening. In the early hours of Monday morning I was again woken by Sonja thrashing about and moaning. Thinking that she was climbing out of bed again, I reacted immediately raising up to first peer across the inky blackness of the room. To my astonishment, the whole of the corner of the room was lit up in a gentle white light. The light was emitting from a being, over six feet tall and seeming to be composed of what looked like electrical energy very like that in a fluorescent tube. The head of the being resembled a muslin bag and bore no features. Around the top of the head was a scroll looking like a roll of material very much like that which an Arab would use to hold on his headdress, but it was a part of the head. The head was the only static part of the being. The body was a band of light possibly a foot wide just below the head and diminishing in width and density towards the floor, fading out about six inches above the floor. The whole of the body was shaking in an exited vibration with waves of movement travelling from top to bottom. The faded lower part was moving with the fastest vibration. The arms were represented by a single band of light at right angles to the body from a normal shoulder position, passing over the upper rail of the bunk bed and appearing to be connected to Sonja's chest. These were vibrating at a much slower rate with gentle waves travelling down them. In the light emitted by this being, I could see Dales's face shining as he lay fast asleep on the lower deck. I could see the whole of the bunk bed and remember the flowered curtains to the left of the bunk shining their colours in the eerie light. Although this description is rather long, all this was observed within seconds. My immediate reaction was:-This is a ghost,belonging to this hotel and it is interfering with my daughter. A wave of anger swept over me and still raising up in bed, I started to say, "Leave her alone." The word "Leave" was hardly through my lips when there was a popping noise and the being disappeared instantly, leaving the bedroom instantly pitch black. Sonja stopped moaning and thrashing about. By this time I was out of bed and crossing the room in the darkness, guided by my memory of the room as I had just seen it. I stood on the spot where the being had been and said with great anger, "Look! I don't know who you are, or what you are, but leave my child alone." I stood for a few seconds then added, "If you want help, then come to me. I will help you all I can, but leave my child alone." I reached out and held Sonja's hand in the darkness and said, "Are you all right, love?" but she was sleeping deeply and peacefully and I realised then, so were Beryl and Dale. Another thing which came to mind as I stood there was the realisation that I felt absolutely no fear. On reflection, I feel that this was because the being appeared to have fled at my challenge. Feeling my way back across the inky black room I found the bedside light and switched it on.

The flowered curtains were the first thing I noticed and the pattern was exactly as I had seen in the light emitted by the being. I must say that I had not taken much notice before. Sonja had kicked off the bed covers with her struggling, so I covered her up and walked down the hotel corridor to the bathroom. I didn't bother with the lights in the corridor even, and realised that I didn't feel at all nervous. When I was back in bed again, my family were all still soundly asleep. As I lay there my thoughts were on what I had seen, my only knowledge of ghosts so called, was that which I had read in Sunday newspapers and kid's comics.

Another thought then crept into my mind..... Twenty years ago, when walking home from my then girlfriends house at 2.00 am. having missed the last tram as usual, I saw what I can only describe as a flying saucer. I told very few people about this as I felt without proof they would not believe me anyway, but it was a very real and frightening experience. As this is another story entirely I will not go into it at the moment, but mention it because it affected my reasoning in the next few weeks. Even as I lay there in bed, the thought started,"Was this a being from another world? Had I seen something which I was not supposed to? Was this in fact a ghost as I had first assumed?" The thoughts went on. The most overriding realisation of all was that I had witnessed a life form, absolutely real and totally different to that of mankind as we see ourselves.

We are not alone, there is other life in the universe, there has to be a God. The thoughts rolled on until I drifted back to sleep.

The following morning we had difficulty waking Sonja, Dale was as lively as ever and I was thankful that he was unaffected by the events in the night. Sonja was absolutely washed out all day and as I watched her sitting lethargically on the beach, I thought, "It is just as if all the spirit has been taken out of her." Beryl noticed Sonja's state and said, "I hope that Sonja isn't sickening for something." I said, "It is possibly a delayed reaction from the journey down, she slept very badly last night, I thought at one point she was trying to get out of bed again." During the night I had decided not to tell Beryl what I had seen until after the holiday, otherwise she might have missed a few nights sleep herself. I kept this from my mother also for the time being.

As I watched Sonja sitting there I wondered if these visits had occurred before and if she knew of this entity. As there were some chalk rocks behind us, I picked up a piece and drew a cat on the concrete sea wall. Pretending to play a game, I said to Sonja, "What is that?" She replied, "A cat." I drew several animals and had similar responses from her. I then carefully drew the entity and said, "And what is this?" She looked slightly puzzled then shrugged her shoulders and said, "It looks like a ghost" Laughing, I said, "How do you know what a ghost looks like if you have never seen one?" She replied, "I have seen drawings of them in comics and library books." It was pretty obvious that she had no awareness of the entity. At home she had her own bedroom and always had a night light so the circumstance of being in the same room as us in the pitch darkness was unusual. I decided to let the matter drop and get on with the holiday.

On successive nights there were no more happenings and rather strangely I felt no apprehension. The rest of the holiday was excellent and Sonja was back to full vigour by Tuesday morning.

After the holiday it was back to work and normal living. I told Beryl about the entity and it didn't seem to worry her too much. She probably thought that I had suffered a vivid nightmare and I must add at this point that it most definitely was not. I have never been a person of wild imaginings and know precisely what is happening around me and as a draughtsman accept nothing without proof. When a fortnight of my normal routine had passed, the materialisation became just an occasional memory and I decided that it was best left as that.

Sonia back to full vigour by Tuesday, on the beach with Dale.

Bebe & Dale, oblivious to all which had transpired.

Back home and using up a snap. Unaware of what was about to begin.

Westgate two years earlier. Dale at 9 months enjoying his first holiday.

One morning I was on my way to work in the car, just a matter of a two mile drive, coming towards me down a quiet back street was another car. It suddenly veered across the centre of the road onto my side and drove straight at me. To my horror I saw that it did not appear to have a driver. I swerved towards the nearside kerb, hitting it with quite a bang. Suddenly the face of the driver of the oncoming car appeared in the windscreen. He had apparently dropped something, probably a cigarette, and spent a little too long trying to pick it up. I laughed later when I remembered the look of horror on his face as he swerved back to his own side of the road, but at the same time my adrenalin rose and I still felt a little dithery an hour later.

As I was working near to home, I used to go home for lunch each day for I had an hour to fill. On my way home that same day, a motor cyclist came straight out of a side turning as I travelled along the main road, and swerved to miss my bonnet. I swerved across the road into the face of oncoming traffic and had to swerve immediately back, just missing the motor cyclist a second time. The motor cyclist scarpered off knowing full well that he was at fault. My adrenalin was up again and I thought, "What a coincidence, twice in one day." After lunch I was driving back to work when a car shot out of a side street stopping half way across my carriageway. Once again I had to swerve towards oncoming traffic to avoid him. This time I stopped and the driver apologised profusely. I realised as I stood there that my legs were very dithery and I thought, "Someone or something is out to get me here!" .....three near misses within a few hours, all definitely not my fault, when I had previously had very few such incidents in all my years on the road on cycles, motor cycles and in cars. During that afternoon at work, my mind kept going back to the entity which I had seen. I knew of no-one who had witnessed anything like it and more and more I thought, "I have seen something which I should not have witnessed, something is out to silence me!" It is difficult to write of these thoughts at a later date, because, with the knowledge which I have gained over the years, the fear I developed seems irrational and childish, but fear is of the unknown. I know now that the fear was developed within me purposely to motivate me against my judgement of forgetting the incident. However, motivated by this fear I started wondering who I could confide in for advice and help.

My mind went back to my previous employer, a large engineering firm in Sheffield, There, a chap called Bill who was in charge of the development workshop was, I had been told, a spiritualist. As I had never discussed this with him, I had absolutely no knowledge what a spiritualist was or what they did. I just thought that perhaps by meeting in each other's houses and sitting around tables holding hands behind closed doors and curtains, that they somehow managed to contact supposed spirit entities to communicate and learn of the other world and maybe their own destinies. None of this had ever appealed to me.

In desperation I phoned Bill and poured most of my fears and experiences down the phone. Bill didn't seem very surprised or excited by what I told him and when I had finished just quietly said, "Why don't you come along to a service at our church and we will see if we can help you." I was mildly surprised to find that spiritualists had churches, with hindsight, I am astonished how I ever missed this. He gave me directions and times and I went to the church the following Sunday, not knowing what to expect. When I walked in it seemed like a normal church service in a small orthodox looking church. I sat on a chair on a row about halfway down the hall, there were perhaps twenty or thirty people there of all types and ages. A lady come onto the rostrum and was introduced as Mrs. H. of a town about one hundred miles away, she seemed to be a stranger to the church as well as to the city of Sheffield. This puzzled me slightly as the Churches which I used to attend usually had their own Minister. Mrs H. opened with a prayer, then a hymn, then philosophy on the transition from the material to the spirit world, another hymn and then the chairman on the rostrum said that Mrs H. would now give a demonstration and proof of communication between the two worlds with our dear departed. She would start off, pointing perhaps to a lady and saying, "I would like to speak to the lady in the blue hat. Yes you dear. I am sorry to point. Would you know an Elizabeth in spirit?" The lady would more often than not say, "Yes." and then , "There is a Tom on your father's side?' "Yes." "And a girl here, about thirteen years old as I see her," the lady would start to shake her head and Mrs H. would continue, "She has grown in spirit and is telling me that she passed over when she was only two years old." There would be great surprise from the lady and recognition of the young girl. Mrs H. would then say, "You are at present looking after an old lady, and feel so tied down and are carrying faithfully on with this work in spite of appearing to receive no gratitude, Tom is saying 'Thank you'." There would be complete agreement from the lady and maybe a few tears. This is not an actual account, but is typical of the messages given by Mrs H. and she spoke to many people, with acceptance and agreement in most cases.

After a while I was quite impressed and gained respect for Mrs. H. I was convinced she would speak to me because every one else's problems seemed so everyday at the side of my happening. Suddenly, Mrs H. said, "God Bless you all." and sat down. There was another hymn and a collection at some point and Mrs H. followed by my friend Bill, who had been playing the organ and hadn't noticed me in the congregation, and several other church members went into a back room and closed the door. The rest of the congregation filed slowly out chatting and laughing together. Still sitting there, I felt quite deflated. How could Mrs H. in such free communication with spirit have missed what had happened to me?

Still desperate for advice and help I went to the door of the back room and knocked. Someone opened the door to reveal about eight people with tea and biscuits. I said, "I am sorry to bother you but Bill asked me to come along as I have seen something and need help." Bill nodded towards me and said, "Oh, Hello there." I smiled at him and still standing in the doorway told them as quickly as possible what I had seen. As I finished, Mrs H. said very angrily, "You people make me sick. You come here blaming us for these things that happen to you and expecting us to sort it all out." I stood there stunned, any respect I had gained went instantly, I had blamed no-one for anything, so I just turned and left the church. For days after I felt quite low and began to pray to God again. I say again because there was a time in my life from about eighteen to twenty four when I felt a duty to pray every night before I went to sleep. This period coincided with falling in love with my wife-to-be and being separated by going into the Air Force, worry about my mother being told she may die of angina and other such emotional happenings and worries. At this time, prayer gave me great comfort, for I had always believed in God. Drifting from regular prayer occurred when I was involved in the material happiness and whirlpool of homebuilding, work, play and marriage. By praying again I started to feel that I had an ally to protect me from whatever.

The episode with Mrs H. confused me for a short time but I decided that the best avenue I had for some sort of help would be through the Spiritualist Church, although I was very wary about who I would listen to, for there are sincere and devout people, but also fanatics, misguided people and those of low mentality in all walks of life, also people with a little knowledge in any topic can be the most dangerous.

Each Sunday I attended the Spiritualist Church, sitting quietly in the centre of the room hoping to be visually conspicuous even if not spiritually conspicuous. The philosophy began to appeal to me and I enjoyed this more than the demonstration which often seemed like fortune telling, this mainly depended on how spiritual the medium was. Each week a different medium, sometimes from the far reaches of the country, would take the service. Most of them were very accurate with the messages they gave, I gained respect again but it was a while before I received a message.

The first contact came in November 1973 when an International medium, Margaret Pearson, took the service. In her demonstration she came to me first, she said, "Do you have anything to do with solicitors, for I see you in this type of surrounding? March next year will see you in a new job in Harrogate." She then said, "There is a dear little lady standing by me, only about so high with a sweet round face and white hair. She is happy in spirit and gives out love and is here to guide and help you. I feel that she died at eighty." I thought, 'Is this mind reading? That is Gran on Mom's side!' She then said, "Do you know a Robert or Bob?" I replied, "No!" She said, "There is also an Alice." (I in fact called to see my mother on the way home, she told me that Bob was her brother who had died whilst I was young and Alice was his wife. This certainly wasn't mind reading for I knew nothing of them.). Margaret Pearson then said,, "I feel that you are going to work in the spiritual field. Would you be happy to travel in this work? I see you travelling a lot in the near future." A few weeks after this message, I bumped into an old friend who said, "I now run a contract design and draughting agency, would you like a job with me, it could involve travelling, but always within easy reach of home? You will be on twice the money you earn at present." I replied, "I will certainly think about it!" He then said, "I have had an enquiry this week for which you have exactly the right experience and qualifications." "Where abouts would I be working?" I asked. "Harrogate." he replied. "How soon can I start?" I asked. "That was quick," he said.

The Secret of Life

When I went to the contract agency office in the centre of Sheffield it was in an old building surrounded by solicitors offices. Margaret Pearson had been spot on.

In this my first message I was expecting all things to be explained to me and on that count alone, I was disappointed. After many successive meetings and after many incredibly accurate messages from many mediums, I began to realise that my answers would come after a slow process of learning; how could colour be explained to the blind, or sound to the deaf? My spiritual eyes and ears had to be opened.

Chapter 2

My Doorkeeper "Che Minh"

As well as I can sketch him: before he materialised to me, I had a mental image of a slim, elegant mandarin Chinaman in embroidered robes and three cornered hat. My heart warmed to the little plump baby faced chap, with the laughing eyes. Full story Chapter 17

The Process of Learning

As the weeks passed, as well as attending services at the spiritualist churches, I began to attend open circles. These were a meeting of any interested parties, the intention being to discover any psychic ability or gift as the older mediums would call it. The circles were controlled by an experienced medium and would usually be attended by other local mediums, so for the lesser experienced, plenty of help and advice was available. We would all sit in a circle usually, but not necessarily, most of us with our eyes closed, trying to clear our minds of material rubbish. Many methods were used to help this meditational state, a more common one was to imagine the flame of a candle or a floating white feather. Thinking of the mind as a mirror whose surface was filled with images created by sound, sight, smell, touch, taste and thought, if all these could be diminished then as the mirror cleared, the spirit guides could inject a thought or image in the space created.

This process did begin to work and when the contact came it was usually brief but recognisable because the image, sound or smell even, was totally alien to ones normal thought processes. The medium in charge would keep asking, "Do you have something?" so that when we had given whatever we sensed, the flow would continue. I know that when I was either nervous or reluctant to speak, the visions would stop for a while.

It became very noticeable to me that the messages which I received from mediums and others were mostly from guides, whereas the bulk of the messages received by others in the circles and church services seemed to be from relatives and friends who had passed over. The person giving the message would usually sense or see the form of a spirit guide standing by me or linked to me in some way, or would hear or sense an identification or message from a guide. At first this sort of message was hard to accept, because often there was no proof, quite unlike being told of a relative or friend of whom the medium could not possibly have prior knowledge, remembering that many of the mediums were total strangers. However after a while a pattern began to emerge, the same guides were given over and over again by totally different mediums in totally different places.

Hagdal And A Monk

The most predominant of the guides was one who showed himself as a Cheyenne Indian Chief's son who gave his name as Hagdal and was frequently described as being about thirty years old, of very stocky build and having unusually dark skin for a Red Indian. He was quite rightly described as being very dominant and aloof and very dedicated to his purpose which was healing.

He said many times that he wished to lead a team of healing guides and that it was very difficult to find a suitable instrument. This being a person in the material world with the right qualifications of love above all and of strength and tenacity and of the right vibration. At first this mention of compatible vibrations puzzled me and one or two mediums who used the term were puzzled by it also.

I began to understand when a medium addressing me from the platform in church mentioned a monk who had been given to me many times and said he was having to work through me from a distance via other guides because his vibration was too high and to use me directly would damage my physical body. He said that if I worked hard to purify my thoughts and deeds then my vibration would rise and he would wait in his timeless state for that condition when he would be able to work through me with great power. This was one of many messages which were given to me in those early years suggesting that I should tidy up my thoughts and actions, quite rightly I suppose, for although there are moments of great compassion, I am certainly no 'Holy Joe' and have always had great respect for those people who seem to always do and say the right thing, personally though if there is any temptation, I usually seem to fall for it.

Che Minh

Many of the guides who were given to me in those early years have since appeared to me and I must add, have sometimes surprised me by being totally different in appearance to the image held in my mind. One such guide is a Mandarin Chinaman, who I call Che Minh. Whether this is his real name, I don't know, but he has never objected. Che Minh was one of the first guides I learned of and is my door keeper. For the uninitiated this means that he vets any entities trying to work through me and will let only those of the right intentions through to my conscience. He has warned me that as I have free will, I can override his good judgement, so to be on my guard at all times during contact with spirits. I don't know what religion Che Minh was in material life but he respects that anyone approaching me from spirit must do so within God's laws and must, as I do, believe in all the teachings of Christ as set down in the James' version of the New Testament.

This is important to me as some updated versions have altered the meaning, and a certain well known religious sect have altered the punctuation and succeeded in reversing the meaning.

On this very important point of acceptance of contact from spirit, St John gives the best advice in his first epistle, Chapter 4, when he says, "Believe not every spirit, but try the spirits whether they are of God." If ever I am approached by spirit entities, which has happened many, many times over the years, I always say through the mind, "God's Blessing be with you; if you come within God's laws and believe in the teachings of Jesus of Nazareth, then you are most welcome: if not, please go your way and I will call my guides to help you in any way you need." This is said through the mind, because I have found out by experience that to speak out aloud during contact instantly destroys the image or communication. The type of contact referred to here occurs mostly during the night in bed, or during private meditation and I do not advise anyone to try to sit for contact alone until they have first gained knowledge and experience with other mediums and can work fully and with great trust with their spirit guides.

Communicating between the two worlds is a very complicated business and depends greatly upon the natural ability of the medium. Many mediums I have met over the years have this natural ability and the messages flow through them easily and freely, although I find it quite surprising that some of them do not seem to understand the source or the mechanics of their gift. Regarding this gift, I greatly admire the persistence of my guides in trying to work through myself; on several occasions they have described working through me as, "Like trying to work through a brick wall."

Taps And Nudges

They did, however, find a means of communication which has proved invaluable over the years: This is a series of taps and nudges about my body. At first, I began to worry because I started getting so many muscle spasms, or so I thought. It seemed that my nervous system was going haywire. Every day there was tap, tap, tap on my right leg, then left leg, right arm, left arm, right shoulder, left shoulder and so on. I hesitated on seeking medical advice because there was a sub-conscious feeling that this was something to do with spirit. It became evident after weeks of this, that when I said or did something right, I would receive a tap or nudge on my right hand side. Something said or done wrong, would result in taps or nudges on my left hand side. I then noticed that the greater the right or wrong then the larger the limb which was nudged.

For example, if I did or thought something very devious, spiritual matters being the last thing on my mind, then I would receive a furious nudging on my left thigh, as if I was being told off. If I made a minor error of judgement, then there would be a tapping on, say, my left forearm etc.

There would be similar effects on my right side for good thoughts or deeds. After the initial surprise, the nudges became almost predictable and I began to think that I was anticipating them if I knew that I was doing right or wrong.

As I stated earlier, my trouble is that I always need so much proof before I will accept anything. It was only when I could rationalise and think back to that very real materialisation from my daughter that I would think, "There is another life form, this is communication," and then for a while I would accept.

At this time I had begun to meditate alone and was getting some very inspiring results, some of these I will mention later. The place I chose for uninterrupted meditation was the loft in my house which is boarded out for storage and I would sit on a stool on top of the trap door so that there couldn't be any sudden interruption. My wife was very understanding of my pursuits, bless her, and probably put it down to the male menopause. Sitting in meditation one evening, I made the point of my meditation , the question of these nudges. I started off with a prayer, then asked God's permission that I could communicate directly with my guides, then I asked Che Minh to please watch over me and allow through only those who came within God's Laws etc.. As I settled into the meditation, I said through the mind, "I am quite concerned about all these taps and nudges, they seem to be a method of communication. With great respect, could you possibly prove to me that this is not just my muscles going into spasm through stress or perhaps some psychosomatic effect?" There was instantly a very strong tapping on my right kneecap. The meditation was over and I was laughing delightedly, the guides had proved their point with great humour - there is no way that this could have been muscle spasm. Now that I had accepted this means of communication it was to prove invaluable in all my future teaching, The brick wall had been breached.

To elaborate on the strength of these nudges an amusing, if not spiritual incident occurred. I sold a car to a friend at work. He had owned the car for about a year when he went out in it on company business. Late in the morning, the phone in the office rang, it was Ken, asking for me. He was phoning from the motorway service area and said that the car engine had seized up. He had somehow managed to get it to the service area but was at a loss as to what to do next, so he phoned me for advice. I told him that the most likely cause was that he had run out of coolant, maybe through a leaking hose. As I said this I received a very strong nudging on my right shoulder. I thought, "The guides are even helping me with material problems now." I then said with great confidence, "This is certainly the case." Ken replied, "The car is just by the phone box, hold the line and I will put another ten pence in and go to look." He came back after a minute and said, "You were right, there is no water at all in there." I asked him when he had last checked it, and eventually with great honesty, he admitted that he hadn't checked it in the whole of the year that he had owned the car. I advised him to let it cool down, fill it with water, check for leaks, then try to start it. I then said, "Cheerio." and put the phone down. As I did this, one of the chaps in the office rushed across to me and said, angrily, "You have let him go! I told you I wanted a word with him about the job and now I have no way of contacting him." I replied, "Well, I didn't hear you above the noise of the machines out there." He said, "Well, I tapped your shoulder hard enough when I told you!" He is probably still wondering today why I found this so funny.

Brain-washing

One of the things which I have always thought to be wrong with religion is the amount of what I would term 'BRAIN-WASHING' in the different denominations - people being given carefully chosen writings by the elders and told to accept nothing else.

Most religious organisations have dogma and creed which is different to the rest. All claim that theirs is the way, some very graciously say we can accept most of 'so and so's teaching, except for.....'. Who is right? They can't all be. My belief is that we should consider all things and choose by free will. Guidance into the most fruitful channels would be a great aid, but whose guidance do we trust in so important a matter. To me, the most important guide is God. The most certain thing I have ever known of God is Love, so if any teaching is of love and compassion, instinctive and without question or compensation, it can be accepted. Therefore, The New Testament seems to me to be the perfect choice. If we could live up to the words of Jesus Christ in the Sermon on the Mount, we would need nothing else.

Having said this, I also believe that there is a need for all the different religions because of the very great differences in people's thought patterns. Some are more direct roads to the truth and our choice depends mainly upon the stage of our incarnations through these lives. So, choose carefully but never condemn anothers choice; theirs may be a more direct road for them.

Books

About a year into my search for the truth, people in all areas of my life - work, play, church, family etc. started handing me books, usually saying, "I thought that you may be interested in this." This was very noticeable as it hardly ever happened before, and after a few years it more or less stopped. I would always accept the book on loan, but would not always read it, for at some time during the consideration to read, I would receive a positive or negative nudge. The encouragement or discouragement did not stop at that, there would be agreement or disagreement in this way on most major points throughout the book.

These books included the Mormon Bible, the Jehovah's Witnesses' Bible, Bhagavad Gita As It Is (Hiri Krisna), books on Spiritualism even on Satanism (my left leg was nearly knocked off), books on Meditation, Trance Addresses, Apports, Production of Ectoplasm, Astral Travel and of course, many versions of the Bible (should I say, my right leg was nearly knocked off)). There were many others too numerous to list.

On only one occasion I can think of did I have the desire to seek and buy a book. These books were often handed to me after a physical, Spiritual or emotional experience and more often than not the explanation would be in the book. The sequence of all this never ceased to amaze me and went way beyond any coincidence. At this point, I would like to say thank you to all those dear friends who were inspired to help me.

Visits - Direct Voice

About this time, there began to be a series of visits in the night by various entities, some of which I will describe later in the book. They came both to help and to be helped. The most important part of the teaching came in conjunction with these visits, and this I think of as the Dream Teachings.

Basically I would be given a dream which was always recognisable by its bright colours. It would be unlike normal dreams or nightmares inasmuch as it would be absolutely rational. When I woke from the dream it would usually be about four in the morning and the whole of the dream would be clear in my mind. I would then make sure that I was fully awake by listening to the ticking of the clock, my wife's breathing and looking around the bedroom in the dim light. Then I would say through the mind, "Was that a teaching dream?" Sometimes I would receive a nudge on my right leg in confirmation and sometimes a direct voice from somewhere in the bedroom would say, "That is so." or "Correct." or "Yesss!" but always would confirm in a different way as if to reassure me that it was not imagination. I told my wife of this voice and I think she only half believed me until she woke one night and heard it for herself. After receiving confirmation of the teaching dream I would go downstairs and write a brief account in my notebook and a very brief interpretation whilst it was still in my mind.

Clairsentience

Another avenue of learning came through private circles, usually by invitation, at the house of a medium. These were excellent for developing clairsentient mediumship, which I think is the mediumship of this age. Basically, rather than seeing or hearing spirit, one almost imagines the contact, consequently until a degree of experience is acquired, there is a fear of looking and sounding foolish. In the private circle this does not matter and the sitter is able to give everything which enters the mind, giving the guides a chance to inject information relating to and to be recognised by other sitters. To my delight I found that I was giving accurate messages which, when I gave them sounded frivolous to me. This clairsentient mediumship was far more fluid and I was delighted to be able to give messages at public meetings with a degree of confidence and accuracy.

The Laying On Of Hands

The primary interest through all this was still healing and upon invitation I had joined a group of healers in a smaller local Church. With this group I learned the physical and ethical requirements of the laying on of hands - basically not to actually touch, but to lay hands on the aura, although I noticed that certain members of the group were literally man-handling people. I can understand this, for in the early stages of healing development there is a feeling of not giving enough and it seems more satisfying to the inexperienced healer to grab and manipulate an arthritic joint. The ethics were basically not to see anyone, either male or female, whilst alone. There were quite a few books on healing passed to me at this time and nudges of agreement or disagreement from my guides steered me into my present methods. Although I still fall into the trap of wanting to give of myself, I am still very aware that the healing guides are the givers and I am just the channel through which the healing flows; in using me they are just obeying a basic physical law. This I will explain more fully in a later chapter.

There began to be a link between the healing and the inspirational mediumship. Some well practiced healers have said, 'Do not mix the healing and the giving of messages', but I found that quite often I would be inspired to tell the patient of things I had sensed when the laying on of hands was finished, whenever this occurred it was always gratefully accepted and I realised that some people simply needed proof of spirit. It could, however, be said that the curing of an ailment should be sufficient proof.

At one point the clairsentient mediumship began to occupy most of my time until the guides contacted me and said, "You have to make up your mind whether you wish to be a healer or a platform medium. The guides who are working healing through you have been with you for a long time and you are far more developed in healing than you realise. If you wish to be a platform medium you have freedom of choice, but you will have to go back to the beginning of the road." I felt quite humble, there was no question the healing mattered more than anything. I was told that the two roads would eventually blend and I would do both, but the healing was to be predominant for quite a while.

By attending the Spiritualist Churches I have made many dear friends, some of them are so gifted that they have my greatest admiration. One thing which I could not accept, however, was that some churches ignore the teachings of Christ and do not have a bible, or show a cross. The members of these churches look on Christ as 'another' medium. Perhaps I am being a little critical or displaying a little dogma of my own, if this is so, then please forgive me, but to say 'another' medium seems to infer 'like I am' and this makes me shudder with humility for I do not feel worthy of fastening the buckle of His shoe. One of my very dear friends, Myra, is a very gifted medium who moved to Sheffield from London for a while. Through the influence of her guides she became an avid reader of the New Testament and would often quote from it. She loves and respects Christ just as I do, and she is a Jewess. There are many churches which class themselves as Christian Spiritualist and they do in fact, use the Bible and display the cross. The one thing I found in all these churches, both Christian Spiritualist and otherwise, was the very great love of God and humanity.

With regard to the healing group which I joined, we did a great deal of good work together and I learned a lot from everyone. Then I started getting nudges on my left leg. This puzzled me for quite a while, until there came a phase where the people who were coming for healing were generally in better condition than I was and were the same people week after week. Many a time I thought, 'It should be me in that chair and this very robust lady or gent giving to me'. This did coincide with a time when I was going through great stress and having difficulty keeping all the balls in the air at once. It was then that I started to feel the healing does not belong just in the Church, it belongs to the people like those who through infirmity cannot get to church, and especially those who through lack of interest or inspiration do not have the comfort of God. It was time to move on. Rather strangely, because this was a major decision, I do not remember any direct message from my guides to do so. This I fully understand now, because the guides will never make a decision which will affect the life experience or Karma of anyone in this plane, because if they do and things go well, theirs is the glory, if things go wrong then theirs is the condemnation.

This defeats God's basic law of personal responsibility. It took me quite a long time to realise that whenever a direct question was asked, affecting decision, there was never an answer. It was only when I had made a decision or performed an action that there would be nudges of agreement or disagreement or the direct voice making comment. There were nudges, however, that seemed to say 'we agree with your thoughts or what is happening, or disagree with your thoughts' etc. Being what I am, many times I ignore the nudges and go ahead with my thoughts or actions anyway.

I think the guides despair of me sometimes, no wonder they once said the right instruments are hard to find.

This chapter has really been a condensed version of the general run or pattern of teachings and accounts for only a small part of what happened over the years, with a few examples of my own views and thoughts which have influenced my choices and actions. I hope from here on to tell of some of the happenings which never ceased to amaze and move me.

Chapter 3

The First Direct Communication
February 1974

The First Direct Communication

Whether it is by coincidence or whether it is because of the proximity of sleeping bodies enclosed within a small area, I cannot really decide, - I think I would go for the latter, but the beginning of the first direct communication with spirit was whilst we were on holiday once again, in August '73.

My family and I were in a caravan on a site at Humberstone near to Cleethorpes. We had taken my mother along with us again, so there were five of us under one roof. On the third night of the holiday I was woken in the early hours of the morning in the grip of a great force. It felt as if a huge suffocating weight was pinning me to the bed, my whole body was sizzling like a piece of bacon in a frying pan,. This was accompanied by complete paralysis. I knew that I was in the grip of some entity. A great feeling of fear and panic welled up inside me. This grew in magnitude with the realisation that I could not breathe. I fought with all my might but could not break free. At the same time I could see the roof of the caravan in the dim light and was aware of my wife Beryl by my side. The main thought in my mind was that if I did not get a breath then I would surely die. If only I could attract Beryl's attention then I felt sure that she could help. I tried desperately to shout 'Bebe', which is my nickname for her. After what seemed like an eternity in this state, my mouth slowly began to move and a low buzzing began through my closed lips. This suddenly released into an explosive shout of 'Bebe!'. Instantly the paralysis was released and a ball of white light left me and went shimmering away through the caravan roof. As I lay there, I could hear my voice echoing through the caravan, but rather strangely, no-one was woken by it. Still in a state of fear, I began to pray to God for help and protection, eventually going back to sleep.

For the rest of the holiday I felt uneasy during the nights, or on occasions when entering the caravan alone in the dark I thought that I sensed a presence. One evening when walking through the caravan alone, a straw hat seemed to fly from the top of the wardrobe, landing halfway down the 'van. It probably just fell off because of the outside door being left open, but in my heightened state of anxiety I was convinced that forces unknown were responsible. As I progressed and learned more of the spirit guides in the months after this visit, the fear began to leave me and looking back, I realise it was the only occasion upon which I have been really afraid. Like all fear, it was of the unknown and was related to having no control over the happening.

After the visit in August '73, there were many minor visits in the night such as nudges and taps and fleeting glimpses of faces, usually upon waking, but nothing to write of at this point. It was in the early hours one morning in December '73 that another powerful visit occurred.

This time I was at home in bed in quite normal circumstances when I awoke in a paralysed state accompanied by the now familiar sizzling and the inability to breathe. There seemed to be a heavy weight on my legs only. The non-breathing I had now become accustomed to, for I found that no matter how long this state seemed to last, it did not cause any real distress or ill effects. Through experienced mediums and reading, I had by now learned to greet the entities, albeit with caution. I would start by saying, "God bless you," then say, "If you come within God's Laws and are here to do God's work or are here for help, then you are most welcome. Otherwise please go your way." However, my mistake then was to try to say this aloud instead of through the mind. Struggling very hard to operate my mouth, I was mindful to check that I was truly awake by staring at the bedroom ceiling, listening to the clock ticking and my wife breathing by my side. There was a feeling of satisfaction that I felt no fear then the words slowly came from my mouth, "Glodd Bress Jooooh!" There was instant release from the paralysis and full.control of my faculties returned. I could still hear my voice uttering these ridiculous words. I became convulsed with laughter and had to get out of bed and go to the bathroom to avoid waking Bebe. The visit was certainly a very uplifting one, whether this was intended or not. After this I realised that absolute calm was essential and only to speak through the mind.

It was February 1974 when the third visit took place. At about four in the morning I awoke in the paralysed state once again, sizzling from head to foot. This time it felt as if a huge weight was on my chest. Gazing calmly at the ceiling in the dim light cast through the curtains from the street lamps outside, I listened to the ticking of the clock and the steady breathing of Bebe by my side. There was the drone of a car going by and fading into the distance. That I could not breathe or move did not matter. I was aware that I was awake and observing all. I greeted the possessing entity, speaking within the mind, "God Bless you; If you come within God's Laws...." Whilst I was going through this greeting, I felt my hands rising beneath the bed covers, they were almost in a position for prayer, just above my chest and about three to four inches apart. As they rose, I realised that I could not feel the weight of the bed covers, in spite of them being heavy winter covers which were tucked under the mattress. Even more puzzling was that although I could see the covers, they were not rising with my hands. However, my hands continued to rise without any direction or effort from me, until my arms felt almost straight. Suddenly, I felt a man's face between my hands, complete with loose skin and bristly cheeks. Still I made no attempt to speak, but heard my own unmistakable voice say slowly and with great emotion, "My father." Then the unmistakable voice of my father said with great warmth and love, "My son." The possession then left me and I was overcome with emotion and began to weep.

When I recovered, there I lay awake, for about an hour and thought back to the two previous very strong possessions and realised that it had been my father trying to contact me. With the first attempt, I realised that not only had I been very inexperienced, but he also, for this was possibly his first attempt. The second time was a little better, but the final contact was great. It was very impressive just how positive the identification had been, even without vision.

All this happened within a year of that astonishing materialisation at Westgate-on Sea and at this point I was beginning to realise that I was not alone in trying to control these contacts but was already aware of a door keeper and many other guides in whom I have great trust, and knew that they were drawing close to do God's work and would not let any disturbed entity through to me. These happenings were being brought to me. In no way was I seeking them. At this stage, I simply tried to understand them as they happened.

At a much later date I understood more of what had happened during my father's third attempt at contact and realise that the reason I could not see my hands rising or feel the weight of the covers was that they were the hands of my etheric body. The hands of my physical body, I am sure, remained on my chest.

The Secret of Life

Thats Dad on the right & Mom, central in white in about 1930. Just back from a tour of the Music Halls in South Africa. As "Eric Briar" and "Jenny Hedge". Didn't the young men look old in those days. Dad was born in 1893 and died aged 78.

Chapter 4

Little Jenny

At 83 years old, outside the flat which she loved so much. Surely one of the strongest people ever to walk the earth. At 82 and suffering angina, bowl cancer and other serious ailments, she came back from death rising over horrific injuries, fighting her way from wheelchair to zimmer to two sticks here and finally to one and normal life. Eat your hearts out you tyrants and bully boys. Her strength was love not hatred and aggression.

Little Jenny

At this point, I feel that I must write of the part that my mother, Jenny, began to play in my understanding of Spirit.

My mother was born into a mining family at Concrete near Rotherham, Yorkshire, in nineteen hundred and three. She had six or seven brothers and sisters and had a very difficult childhood due to poverty and her father being an alcoholic and quite violent at times, often beating my grandmother, which was witnessed with horror by my mother as a child. In the truly classical way, Gran stayed loyal and loving to my Grandad until one morning she woke very early and saw the figure of Christ framed in the bedroom window. She jumped from bed and ran all the way to the pit gates, arriving just before the siren started to sound, signalling an accident. Grandad had been crushed in a roof fall.

Rising over this very difficult start in life, my mother learned to sing and dance and all in spite of being only four feet ten inches tall. She took to the stage at the age of twelve, joining a revue. Through the stage, she eventually met my father, also a stage artist, forming a double act, first as acrobatic dancers, then song and tap.

At the outbreak of World War Two they had my sister, Irene, who was eight at the time, myself who was then five and my brother John who was two. My brother Douglas was due to be born on the night of the Sheffield Blitz, but my mother went out of labour when a bomb hit the house as we all sat on the cellar steps, unable to get to an air raid shelter because of flying shrapnel outside. Douglas was born a fortnight later. There was another sister, Muriel, born in 1943. She died when just a few months old, caused, I was told, by a disease brought by the district nurse, owing to the scarcity of antiseptic due to the war. I can still remember my mother's tears as she tried to bathe her dying child with warm water and cotton wool and the skin slid off the baby's fingers like taking off a glove.

The war and family more or less ended my parent's stage career. They both took jobs in local engineering firms but still did Working Men's club turns in the evenings, quite often for charity. These are just a few facets of my mother's life, towards the end of which she became recognised as the greatest and most stubborn little fighter that most of us had ever met. All in

A much travelled photograph of Jenny aged 14, with the Revue in Ireland. As "Doris De Rose", singing "Deep in the heart of a rose" saved from certain injury or death by her psychic awareness.

all, my parents lives were so full of colour and every possible emotion that it would take volumes to describe the little I know. My mediocre life pales into insignificance when compared with theirs.

There was a happening in my mother's life which showed that she had psychic awareness, although this was the only time which she spoke of in her early life.

What happened was during the fourteen-eighteen war, when she was about twelve or thirteen years old. She was on the way to Northern Ireland to join a revue and was in the care of a Nanny or minder belonging to the same revue. When they were due to board the ship, Little Jenny, as she was then, went into hysterics and would not go on board, resisting to such an extent that the ship left without them. The ship was torpedoed by an early German submarine, sinking with great loss of life.

In the early part of 1974, my mother, then 71 years old, observed the inevitable changes in me, due to the things I have so far described. I had told her of the visits and I think that she received this as most people would, as figments of my imagination. One day she said to me, "Why don't you forget all this stupidity and be happy-go-lucky again, go to the pub with your brothers and have a good laugh. Mixing with all these spiritualists and such people is sending you peculiar."

At this time she was slowly going blind due to glaucoma and had been told that she would shortly have to have her left eye removed. The thought of her beautiful world being turned black destroyed me emotionally. There was nothing she loved more than to be able to walk to the local pub and sing to the people there, accompanied by the piano. I have seen big, strong men weep when she sang 'Sunshine of Your Smile' in her still beautiful voice. She was a true pro'.

By this time I had some experience in the laying on of hands and so wanted to try to heal her eyes, but I knew that she would not sit for me. One Sunday night I prayed with all my heart that her eyes should be healed, but felt that absent healing would not be effective enough. The following afternoon was a holiday and I went to my mother's with my wife Beryl, to fit a carpet. When we walked into the flat, my mother was so

Jenny in the early "Roaring Twenties", as "Dinky Darling" in the "Dinky Darling Revue".

excited to see us and her words were, "Oh Edwin, the most amazing thing happened to me last night. Three of your friends from Spirit came to see me in the early hours of the morning." At this point I interrupted her because I was startled by what she said. If I understood her properly, this was outside my experience, but I was more concerned by the fact that Beryl was with me and although I used to tell her of most things, this sounded a little frightening. I said, "Mom, could you tell me about it when Beryl isn't with me?" Beryl said, "No, let her carry on Edwin." My mother said, "Yes, listen will you Edwin. Three of them woke me up and asked me to sit up in bed. So, I propped up my pillows and sat back. I didn't hear their voices, but I knew what they were saying." I interrupted again, as I was so surprised by Mom's sudden change of heart. I said, "Are you sure that you weren't dreaming?" Mom said impatiently, "Of course I wasn't dreaming, now listen will you! They came towards me in the darkness and I could only see three faces. The centre face at first looked like a skull, but as he came closer he looked like a Red Indian, but with a very dark skin. The one to the right was European and wore glasses and the one on the left had a short white beard."

On hearing this I was quite stunned because she had described exactly three of the healing guides who had been seen close to me by several mediums over the last few months, and I had never told my mother about them. I found myself saying, "Weren't you frightened?" She replied, Of course not," then carried on, "The eyes of the one in the centre appeared to light up and then a round disc, like a magnifying glass, appeared in front of him, focussing the light into my eyes, especially the left one. My eyes started to hurt, but without speaking they said, 'Do not worry, the pain will get no worse than that.' Then the tears started to pour down my cheeks, soaking into my nightie and running around my neck into the pillow. I do not know how long this lasted, but eventually they started to fade and as they reached the end of the bed all three smiled and nodded. I smiled back and said thank you. And thank you Lord God and dear Jesus for helping me." By this time both Beryl and I were lost for words and my Mom carried on, "I reached up and put on the light then found my glasses. It was five o' clock in the morning. I felt so wide awake and bright. My nightie was soaked and so was the pillow so I got out of bed and put on clean ones, then went through to the kitchen and made a cup of tea. I went back to bed but was too wide awake to go back to sleep. I have felt very good all day and my eyes are a lot easier."

At this time I had not seen any of these guides and had to accept what mediums had told me completely independently of one another. Pretty good proof in itself, but this happening left me with no doubt at all. When these guides did manage to show themselves to me as I developed more, the recognition was instant and I knew it wasn't my imagination. The dark skinned Indian was Hagdal, the Cheyenne Chief's son; the one with the white beard I know as von Ericson who was a German doctor and X-ray specialist; the one with glasses was a consultant eye specialist in this life but I do not know his name or nationality, but he only looks about twenty eight or so. I would like to add at this point that identification of the guides is not essential to the healing process and I am sure that many names were given just to satisfy human interest.

In all the information which I gathered on spiritual healing either from books or from other healers, at this stage in my experience, this was the first case I had encountered where the guides had shown themselves to the patient. This happened several times with different patients over the years to date and the reasons for the appearances are not always obvious to me, but I am certain there is a definite purpose either affecting the life of the patient or sometimes acting as a moral booster to myself. In my mother's case, the reason soon became evident.....

Almost every day after that first miraculous visit, she was visited by spirit guides and friends from the past. Always, the visits were controlled and with no disturbed entities. She had in fact, with that first healing, been given the most amazing gift of clairvoyance which I have ever encountered, and which was to sustain her through the very difficult years yet to come. Her first seventy years had been incredibly tough, but that is another story. One thing is certain, she earned the comfort she derived from this whole world of new friends which had opened up to her; and what friends they were. Incredible is an understatement.

One thing which I must clarify before I go on any further and ask to be forgiven if I repeat myself, is that unless a person has seen spirit, it is impossible to describe the reality and the total difference to a dream state. The most difficult person to try to convince would be someone trained in psychiatry, where things are related to the ramblings of the brain.

The Egyptians

The first visit of the incredible new friends came within a few days of the awakening of Mom's psyche. She was woken in the early hours of the morning to find a whole group of entities standing around her bed. She said, to her they looked like Egyptians, but were more beautiful than any person she had seen on this earth. Their hair was jet black and their skin was a shining golden brown.
Most of them seemed to be men, but the most predominant one amongst them was an incredibly beautiful young woman with shining raven black hair, thick and straight around her face with a straight fringe just above her eyebrows. They were all dressed in exquisitely ornate robes, encrusted in gold and jewels, which flowed around them as if they were spun from gossamer, and all wore exquisite golden headdresses encrusted with jewels.

Without saying a word to her they emitted an air of great spirituality and my mother said she felt very small and grubby as she sat up in bed to receive her amazing visitors. As if she had instantly picked up on these feelings, the young woman shook her head slowly and held out her hands in a friendly gesture towards Mom, who felt a great warmth and love from all of them. The 'Egyptians' as Mom called them paid her many visits, right to the end of her life.

The 'Egyptian Girl' as I came to call her, was often seen close to me by many mediums and I felt very happy to have her as a guide. It was certainly very flattering to have the interest of so beautiful a lady. I am sure that she would have been the first to tell me that true beauty is of the soul, not of the appearance. The Egyptian Girl did at a later date appear with two other healing guides to a young woman with very severe cancer in her bones, who I was attending with healing. Also the wife of one of my work associates, about one week after he brought her to me for healing. This certainly was good confirmation of her reality because I hadn't told either young woman of her.

Many mornings of Mom's life she was woken by hosts of spirit entities of all nationalities, who gave her huge bunches of flowers and huge smiles. Regarding the amazing gift of clairvoyance she had received, it was as if the percentage of her material sight which had been lost, had been replaced by the ability to see life in the etheric. The visits to Mom were not all goody-goody however, and two visits where she was reprimanded spring to mind..... Mom had for many years taken snuff, which I have no doubt, she was addicted to. Her addiction started when she had been trying to work on stage, many years earlier in her double act with Dad, and her singing was affected by very severe sinus trouble. An old man in the audience went backstage during the interval and offered her a pinch of snuff. The effect was so good that she was almost back to normal for the next act and she took snuff ever since. During a visit by the the Egyptian guides, the young Egyptian woman stared at Mom with a stern look on her face, then pretended to take a pinch of snuff. She then pointed at Mom and shook her head slowly. Although Mom felt quite humiliated, she carried on with her snuff and I am convinced that it was the cause of the bowel cancer which caused her so much distress from then on.

Another night after Mom indulged in a good drinking spree with my sister Irene, she woke up expecting to see her friends. A loud voice from the darkness of the room said very sternly, "Your breath smells!" Again she felt very humiliated, but didn't give up having a drink. Boy! do I take after her when it comes to learning lessons!

It wasn't very long before my father, who had died about three years earlier, before all this began, took advantage of Mom's new gift and paid her a visit. Without wishing to be macabre, one of the things which had bothered Mom about Dad's passing was that when we paid our last respects to his body, she noticed that his eyelids had sunk and so assumed that his eyes had been taken, possibly for corneal grafts. This seemed to upset her greatly as she frequently mentioned his missing eyes.

One night, just weeks after the firsts visit, she woke up to find Dad sitting on the edge of the bed. He was dressed in his old striped pyjamas, as if to appear at home in the bedroom. As Mom woke, Dad stood and turned to face her. He then held out his hand and said, "Feel my hand Iris." (which he had always called her). She reached out and took his hand and found it to be strong, warm flesh. She had noticed that the bed springs rose as he stood up, indicating weight. He then said, "I love you Iris, look at my eyes." She looked into his eyes and saw that they were bright and sparkling and full of life. She said, "Oh, thank God you have your eyes back." Dad then smiled and left her.

A few nights later he returned and brought with him a young woman who stood nervously behind him. Taking her hand, he pulled her gently forward and said, "I would like you to meet Mary. She is in my choir." Mom said she felt a wave of jealousy sweep over her as she thought, 'He is still womanising, even over there.' When he had gone, Mom felt quite ashamed and asked for God's forgiveness. With hindsight she felt much happier for Dad with the realisation that he was already forming new interests, with a link still to entertainment.

Rescue Work

I mentioned earlier that I do not believe that the spirit guides spend great effort nurturing someone on this plane without good reason.

The reason for their efforts with Mom soon became evident. She woke early one morning to find her whole bedroom full of young children sitting around her in circles, watching her intently. As her main gift was clairvoyance she only heard clairaudiently on odd occasions, so the explanation for the children was given through her mind. They were all children who had passed into spirit in very tragic circumstances and obeying the law of free will were refusing to leave the aura of the earth plane. This was not through childish stupidity.

It must be remembered that the free spirit of a child has the same intelligence as the free spirit of an adult. Christ spoke to this effect when he said, "Except you be as little children, you shall not find the Kingdom of Heaven." The children were drawn strongly to the love of their earth parents from whom they had been so tragically torn and so refused to travel on. It seems that they will consider the reasoning of someone on this plane in this situation more than the reasoning of the guides.

That is where Mom came in. She knew exactly what to do and say, and explained to the children that in their timeless state, their parents could be with them in what seemed 'an instant'. She was inspired to say much more to them and gave out great love and warmth. The children responded by blowing her kisses and went peacefully on their way. Mom was so moved that she wept again as she recounted this to me.

I was no stranger to this work, the old mediums call it 'Rescue'. Mom, on the other hand, knew nothing of such things, it was just automatic to her. After this, she had many people brought to her and she knew just what to do and say and most important of all, she radiated great love to them. To illustrate the great variation of the entities she was called on to help, one night a group of world war two airmen were all around her bed. They wore sheepskin jackets and had leather helmets upon their heads, some still wore goggles and radio gear. They were all of one intention and were chanting, "We want revenge. Kill. Kill." Mom started to try to pacify them in her usual way and upon hearing her voice, they all turned their angry faces towards her. Two of them came towards her in a very menacing way. As they scowled into her face and reached towards her, she said that she became quite frightened for the first time, but carried on appealing to them to pray to God and accept the help of the guides. Eventually they began to listen to her and she explained to them how their hatred had trapped them between the two planes. Slowly they calmed down and listened to her then went their way. Afterwards Mom said that she had been rather annoyed at being frightened in this way and spoke out directly to spirit asking that it shouldn't happen quite like that again.

Shortly after this disturbing visit she became aware of another guide who became the most predominant of all. He was a classical clown, or Columbine and would just materialise by the wardrobe. Mom described him as being over seven feet tall and he would lean on the top of the wardrobe on his right elbow. He wore white tights and pantaloons, a white top with red buttons, and on his head a conical hat in white with a red pompom on top. He never spoke, but mimed in a most amusing way and became a delightful friend to Mom. At some point she realised that he was her door keeper. I explained the role he played in her protection and always after this she felt safe and confident. The clown came to her most nights, no matter who else was there.

Throughout her seventies, Mom became a good companion to me as well as a mother. She began to attend the Spiritualist Church with me and even attended quite a few circles. She was never carried away by it all though, and more often than not would ask to be dropped off at the pub on the way home, so that she could join my sister Irene and her husband for a drink, a sing-song and a good laugh.

Mom, in her mid seventies and enjoying much improved eyesight, finds an outlet for her zest for life, as a television documentary team film, in her pub The Punch Bowl and she quickly gets in on the act.

Throughout these years she suffered a great amount of mental stress, trying to cope with family and other problems, and cope she did. Her eyes were so improved that she was able to have corneal grafts and I remember the tears welling to my eyes as she put on her new glasses and looked out of the window of her flat. She said, "Oh look at the beautiful little birds hopping about in the grass, I didn't realise they were there."

There were however, many other health problems during these years. Some old complaints and some due to the ageing process. She began to sit for healing through myself and as well as the sessions being very successful and helpful to Mom, which was the original intention, they became invaluable to me in the learning process.

I would sit Mom in a comfortable meditational posture with her eyes closed and then begin the laying on of hands. Mom would immediately begin to see the etheric counterpart of the room we were in and as the healing progressed, she would describe the guides as they approached us to do their good work. Often she would describe the room as being full of healing guides, ranging from Indians to Europeans, Monks, Nuns, Gurus, doctors and nurses etc.

It soon became evident that there was a pattern to the healing. Hagdal, the Cheyenne Indian would enter first and would stand at the back of the room, watching very intently. When my hands went to Mom's eyes, the young blond haired man with glasses on would stand before her. He would often look into her eyes using the glass which Hagdal had used on that first occasion. When I went to the area of her hiatus hernia, she would see the young man step aside and a middle aged bald gent in a white smock take over, he looked like a doctor.

As I took the healing to her stomach, I would normally kneel and an old Red Indian with a broken nose and two feathers in the back of his hair would take over - he seemed to be a specialist in bowel disorders. Mom would describe him as kneeling also. When I moved to the arthritic area on her left leg, a large gent with a bushy black beard would take over, he had in fact, given his name through one or two mediums who had seen him with me, as von Heidreich. Two mediums described him as an orthopaedic surgeon during the reign of Queen Victoria.

As I complete a healing session I always feel that I must take the patients hands, during which time I thank God for what has transpired and ask that the healing carry on. At this point, Mom would see Hagdal step forward and take her hands, and all the other healers would step back respectfully. Mom and many other patients would say that during the holding of hands they would begin to tingle slightly and feel as if they were rising up off the seat. I too would often, but not always, feel as if I was floating upwards. Nearly all the guides that Mom used to see, I already knew either by personal visions or through other mediums. It was proof indeed when Mom told me of them without prior knowledge. Her description of their individual speciality I just accepted, for she had given me proof enough.

Over the years, her descriptions of the guides and the duties which they performed reinforced my confidence and my belief. The guides mentioned here are but a few of the total number.

For many years, Mom would put her hand to the area of her appendix and say, "There is something here, you know." She was suspicious that she had a growth of some sort in her stomach. She told the doctor, but he didn't think so. When Mom was about 73, her bowel began to block and the hospital confirmed that there was a cancerous growth. She had been right all along. This type of cancer at her age, didn't normally develop as fast as in a younger person, so we were not unduly worried, but I concentrated the healing to this area and asked that if it was God's will, then it would be removed by a little miracle, but as miracles occur only in special circumstances I asked that at least we should be able to control its growth so that it didn't interfere with her life span or cause too much discomfort.

One of my guides, Saul, was a Moslem in this life and he gave me an old Moslem saying'Mohammed said, "Ask of Allah, but first tie up your camel".' I have adopted this philosophy to this day and I am sure that it is right. It means that we should do everything humanly possible to rectify all situations and only then pray for help. I have seen so many people pray for help at the slightest sneeze and wonder why their cold doesn't go. In Mom's case, the tying up of the camel was the sensible regulation of her diet and the regulation of opening medicine. I kept control of her dosage and a check on the state of her bowel until she was eighty two years old. She had been told that as she had a record of angina, which went right back to her mid forties it was too risky to operate. At 82, a tragic turn of events changed all this:-

All events cast a shadow before them, this shadow can often be seen by a good medium.

It is strange how many things of significance have happened to me whilst on holiday, but, we were all on holiday, that is my family and Mom, when a true Romany Gipsy knocked on the door of the holiday chalet. She offered to tell my fortune, for a fee. As I am not too interested in fortune telling, I declined the offer as politely as possible, for I instinctively knew that she was a true medium and did not wish to hurt her feelings. I did appreciate that she had a living to make and so bought a small trinket from her, paying more than she asked. She promptly proceeded to tell my fortune anyway and was incredibly accurate about cars and houses and work and hobbies and other trivia. She did finally say though, "You are very concerned about someone and are convinced they are going to die, but do not worry, they will not." My thought was,'If she is referring to Mom, she is way out there, we will keep her going for years yet.'

A few weeks after the holiday, on Saturday 8th June 1985 to be exact, I was helping the old lady next door by sorting out the overgrown bushes at the top of her garden. At the time I was aware only of what I was doing - there were no nudges or feelings of impending tragedy, just a pleasant awareness of the hot sun and of the pleasure of the work.

Suddenly, my wife Beryl shouted across the gardens, "Edwin, your mother's been hit by a car and rushed to hospital. Your sister Irene is on the phone. She is very upset, it is very serious," By this time I was across the gardens and over the wall to the phone. Poor Irene. She was almost in hysterics. She managed to tell me that Mom had joined her for a lunch time drink in their local pub 'The Punch Bowl'. She had left early to go home for lunch. As her eyesight was pretty good now, she was in the habit of travelling the quarter of a mile on the bus which went just two stops - door to door. She was always very careful crossing the road so there was no problem there. Apparently she had been standing at the bus stop about five minutes when a seventeen year old youth took the nearby corner at high speed in a car, lost control, shot across the pavement and hit mother square on, crushing her through a fence and down a bank.

I immediately set off for the hospital, in the grip of that strange feeling of numb horror, which anyone who has suffered such a tragedy will know so well. Time seems to stand still and nothing else in the world matters. On the way there, I passed the scene of the accident - the car was halfway up a lamp standard and the broken fence was strewn all down the grassy bank. People still stood in stunned silence as the police interviewed the driver who was apparently unhurt. None of it mattered, I just had to get to Mom.

When I reached the hospital I met my sister, Irene, and my brothers John and Douglas, united in our shock and grief. Mom was still in the early treatment room, she was alive but in a critical condition. After what seemed like an eternity, a quiet middle aged doctor came out to us. His face was very grave. He said, "Your mother has very serious injuries. Up to now, we have found that her left femur is shattered into six pieces;the left shin bone is broken; her right femur has one clean break;her pelvis is broken; her left collar bone is broken and she has a fractured skull. She has serious injuries to the internal tissues and severe external lacerations. The most serious thing of all is that she has lost almost all her blood internally and this alone. a young man of twenty five would have difficulty surviving, you say Jenny is eighty two! You understand what I'm saying don't you? I am most terribly sorry. We are taking her through to the operating theatre now, so would you like a brief word with her?" I said, "Do you mean that she's conscious?" He said, "She has been talking and laughing with us, she is the most amazing person."

We followed the doctor through to the early treatment room, to be met in the corridor by the trolley with Mom on it, already on the way to the operating theatre. We all rushed across to her. Her eyes were closed. I sought her hand and said, "Mom, we are all with you." She looked up and smiled and said, "Oh dear!what a thing to happen." I could not hold back the tears and asked if she was in pain. She just replied quietly, "Of course." and closed her eyes. Then she was taken into the operating theatre. The four of us were left standing in the corridor, just looking helplessly at each other. I am sure that at that moment, any one of us would gladly have changed places with her. The thought of that frail little body suffering so much damage was hard to bear. We were advised not to wait at the hospital, but to phone after10.00pm. so we all made our way home and I for one felt as if I was deserting her. When I arrived home I found a little brass pixie in my pocket and threw it in the bin - so much for the Gipsy's prediction.

After working for Mom's health for all these years, she was now on the verge of death.

When I phoned the hospital, I was told that Mom was still unconscious and in intensive care. All this time I had been praying with every quiet moment, for her recovery. Asking God that the healing guides may be with her constantly to pull her through and ease her pain, shock and discomfort. It crossed my mind that I was praying for Mom to survive in the body, possibly with great disabilities and constant pain. Was this a selfish prayer? Was I praying to avert my own loss? Surely having seen what I had over the last few years, I knew that life is indestructible and that the next state is far better than this! I had also learned that life on this plane is vitally important to the progression of the soul and we possibly learn more in a day on Earth than we do in a year in spirit

Upon leaving the operating theatre, Mom stayed unconscious and in intensive care for four days. During this time, the close family visited at every opportunity. On the fourth day the doctor told us that if her heart and lungs did not work independently of the machine, then eventually she would have to be detached anyway. We had all been encouraged to talk to her and on that fourth day, my wife Beryl and daughter Sonja were with me. I was speaking to her mainly through the mind. Suddenly she said, "Edwin." then she opened her eyes and looked around. We shouted to the nurses, "She has come to." Four of them rushed across and joined us around the bed. Mom looked at the nurses in their white uniforms and smiled sweetly saying, "Am I in heaven?" The nurses all broke into delighted laughter. When they checked Mom's functions, her heart, lungs and nervous system were working perfectly.

Most important of all, her mind was clear and she was able to converse with us straight away. She remembered all details of the accident with great calm and clarity. We had to cut that particular visit short because the intensive care team had a lot of work to do. I did find out though, that during the time in the operating theatre the surgeons had only done emergency repair work, plus putting a pin in the straight forward break in the right femur. There was a long way to go yet.

When Beryl and I visited the following day, Mom was in a room by herself and was quite bright but still very weak. We were told that the doctor in charge was waiting now for her strength to build up before attempting to repair her left femur. I made a point of mentioning to the sister in charge that Mom had bowel cancer and told her of the battle we had to keep her bowels open. She did not seem too concerned. The next time I visited, for some reason I was alone and as I sat quietly with Mom I was able to concentrate more on asking for healing for her. I always maintain that healing comes from God, but know that it is administered by spirit entities who are dedicated to that work and that absent healing is always effective, but it does seem that some essence is passed through the medium here on earth when it becomes necessary, maybe to obey a physical law.

As this was the first chance, since the accident, I took Mom's hands to at least try to pass her some strength. When the praying was through, she looked at me and said, "Edwin, I have something very important to tell you."

"When they were operating on my poor old body, I died, but I have chosen to come back. It all started when I found myself high in the air over the operating theatre, watching the doctors and nurses working on my body." I wasn't surprised when she said this, for I was beginning to realise her recovery seemed to be disobeying all natural laws. She had become such a free traveller between the two worlds over the last few years that she had developed a great sense of awareness and mental control in both the physical and the etheric state.

Mom carried on with her account, "As I watched I heard a droning sound and found myself moving away until I was out of sight of the theatre, in what seemed to be a lift or carriage in a tunnel. I was sitting to one side and as I looked around me I realised that there were one or two others in the same compartment, both adults and children. Some of them were shocked and frightened. I spoke to them to reassure them that all was well and they became calm. Also with us was a little dog which was very frightened, so I picked it up and nursed it and the compartment droned on and on for what seemed like an eternity. Suddenly we were free of the compartment and passing through a vast hall. All around there was peaceful music and clear fresh soothing air. The light was gentle and bright and seemed to come from everywhere. I became aware of people standing all around, looking and reaching towards me. Then I saw their faces and recognised them all. The first was my mother, God bless that sweet little lady, then I saw all my friends from my childhood and I was a child again. All my family and neighbours were there, rather strangely though, I did not see any of my theatrical friends which surprised me, for so many of them have materialised to me at home. I then passed into a room. There was a balcony all around and I was surrounded by white figures who sang like a choir. I then found myself on a bed which began to move towards a slab, to separate the soul from the body.

I pulled the bed back and shouted 'NO! The people in white gowns tried to get me onto the slab again. I resisted and a voice said, "She is over eighty." I shouted, "I am not old, I do not think old." Then I was moving down a corridor again and a huge screen appeared before me. The screen cleared and a figure appeared to one side. It was a young looking man in white robes, he had long white hair and a white beard. He wore golden sandals and there was a slim golden belt around his robe. I thought, 'He is a very ancient holy spirit.' I was overwhelmed by a deep and very emotional love, accompanied by a feeling of awe. I reached out my hands towards him and one of his disciples pulled back his sleeve to reveal his extended hand. I reached out to grasp it and felt a tremendous peace begin to settle over me. But then I thought, 'No. I have so much to do yet.' I began to pull my hands back against quite a strong resistance and the Christ-like spirit smiled gently and said, "So be it. This is the second time that you have refused." Then I began to travel back down the corridor and could hear all the disciples singing in beautiful harmony.

As I passed back through the vast hall, my parents and friends all said, "Oh dear! Oh dear!" as they realised that I wasn't joining them. As I entered the long tunnel all the disciples were singing 'Show me the way to go home, I'm tired and I want to go to bed.' The journey back was very tiring and seemed to go on for an eternity. Every minute of the way I had to battle to keep going. It was me alone against the resistance of travel. The further I went, the greater the droning became and I started to be aware of pain and great tiredness, but I knew that I had to keep going and not slacken in my determination for one second, otherwise, I would slide away again. I must get back, there are so many things left undone. My own voice was ringing through my mind saying,'Oh dear! how much longer the journey is this way.' Suddenly I was back over the operating theatre and the surgeons were walking away from the operating table. A nurse wheeled a trolley alongside and other nurses started to lift my little body from the operating table to put it on the trolley. I knew that if they did, I could not get back. I began to scream at the top of my voice, 'No wait, I am here.' Suddenly one of them said, "She is alive."

They put my body back on onto the table and started to connect things to it and I felt myself falling with a huge thud. After this there was a great blackness until I heard your voice and when I opened my eyes everything was blurred and I didn't know where I was." I said to her, "You thought you were in heaven when you saw the nurses, also of course, you did not have your glasses on. You did, however, seem happy enough with the situation, which surprises me slightly after the fight to get back which you just described." She said, "Well, I knew that things were right whatever because my mind felt so cosy."

It was two weeks after my mother had told me of this remarkable experience, that I was with her when the surgeon came to her with some young doctors. The surgeon introduced my mother to the students saying, "This is Jenny. Our little miracle."

When the surgeon had finished describing the details of Mom's injuries, Mom said to him, "I would like you to meet my eldest son Edwin." I said, "Hello." and thanked him for all he had done for Mom. Then I asked him if he had heard Mom's account of her experience. He said, "No, but I would be most interested to. We are well ahead of schedule this afternoon." Mom gave a slightly abbreviated account of her passing and coming back into the body. When she had finished, the surgeon sat on the edge of the bed looking quite stunned for several seconds, then he said, "The events you described in the operating theatre are exactly as they happened. I have read of this, but this is the first time that it has happened within my experience, that is, for someone to come back with such a clear account." He thanked Mom for telling him. The student doctors were very quiet, so I don't know what their reaction was.

Although what I have just recounted sounds like relaxed and cosy chat between Mom and I, it was anything but. She was not out of the wood by a long way yet. Her situation at this point was that her right leg was repaired with a steel pin and plate, but still had a large operating wound in the process of healing; her left leg was in traction to prevent the muscles contracting onto the six shattered pieces of her femur, some of which had burst through the skin and were in disarray; her left shin was still broken and had been drilled through under local anaesthetic for the traction anchor pin, just above the break. Her pelvis was cracked in several places, but would fortunately repair without further attention. The fracture in her skull was also uncomplicated and would repair itself although the head wound made it very uncomfortable for Mom to rest her head on the pillows, also the broken collar bone made it very difficult to lift her, as most lifting is usually done under the armpits. The multiple lacerations had been stitched and patched and apart from those on her left thigh, were healing well.

She was by now back onto solid food and I was very anxious about her bowel cancer. The reason for my anxiety reached a head a few evenings later, when I received a phone call at about ten in the evening. It was the ward sister, she said, "I am sorry to say your mother has become very ill. The swelling in the tissue around her pelvis, caused by the cracks in the bones, has added to the blockage caused by the cancer and her bowel is blocked completely. She is in great pain and we are preparing her at the moment for an emergency colostomy. Our specialist surgeon is on the way to the hospital now. We have no choice and are very worried about operating in her very weakened state, apart from the complications of all her other injuries." I said, "Have you explained this to my mother?" She said, "Yes. Her reply was "Then get on with it, love, there's plenty of fight in me yet'." I said, "Then she has given the go ahead. Thank you for letting us know." That night there was little sleep for me. I concentrated on praying for help and asked of God that the healing guides may be with her to bring her through this new ordeal. I phoned several times and finally learned that she was out of the theatre and resting comfortably. When I realised how exhausted I felt, it was beyond my comprehension where Mom got the physical strength from to see her through her night.

As the days went by, her colostomy worked well and she gained strength and the orthopaedic surgeon came back to her and said, "We will have to operate on your left leg if we are to save it. If we leave it much longer, the bones will not knit together." Mom said, "You go ahead love, what will be will be." As the surgeon walked away, Mom suddenly saw the Christ like figure with the white beard following him. The figure stopped and turned to look intently at Mom, then he smiled and slowly nodded. Mom shouted after the surgeon, "Don't worry about me, love. God is looking after me." The surgeon operated on her the following day. She was very poorly after the operation and I became very worried about her mind, as for days she said very strange things and hallucinated badly. This made me realise that the mind is the most important part of the human being and if it cannot express itself through an undamaged brain, then all is lost. My anxiety was unfounded.

The old sparkle came back after about a week and Mom began to joke about her new toy. She called it her xylophone. Because Mom had to be moved frequently owing to all her injuries, she could not be put into static traction, so the surgeons had skewered each piece of loose bone in her thigh and brought pins out through the flesh on her leg, linking them together externally. Mom was fascinated with this and played tunes on the pins with a teaspoon. During the many months of recovery, she became well known in the hospital for her sense of humour, her wit and determination. All the younger orthopaedic patients will remember her for her composition during the long periods they were left sitting on bedpans. She called it 'THE BEDPAN SONG'. Copies of her words were passed around and they all used to sing in unison. The hospital, a place of suffering, became a place of laughter.

At eighty three, she learned to walk again with a frame and I remember her joy when she was discharged with frame and wheelchair back to the flat which she loved so much. My wife and my sister, Irene, took to caring for her and she learned to cope with the colostomy. It was a great day when she finally had her first outing to her beloved pub 'The Punch Bowl' with her best pal, my sister Irene. They were more like sisters than mother and daughter. I visited her most nights and continued with the spiritual healing which had sustained her so well.

As I was still a contract draughtsman, I managed to arrange jobs close to home so that I could nip to my mother's in the lunch time and run her to the 'Punch Bowl' to meet Irene. We established a pattern of life and Mom and I grew spiritually together. It was a great day when she put the walking frame to one side and was able to walk just with a stick.

During this time I fought for compensation for her, and when a sum was finally awarded, which was quite moderate in view of her age, she had a bank account for the first time in her life. Rather strangely for someone with new found independence, she wasn't interested in spending the money and used only what was absolutely necessary for holidays with Beryl and me, and Christmas presents etc.

One evening, when she had been sitting for healing with me, she was very distant and said, "Edwin, I would like you to listen for a moment. It was to help Douglas, John, Irene and yourself that I did it." I said, "I know Mom, knowing what we do, I suspected that for a while, but could hardly believe it. You are wrong with me though, for I do not really need any help." She said, "I know that, but you shall be treated equally. When I die, I want you to have equal shares of the compensation. I trust you to arrange all this."

To explain all this, it is quite common knowledge amongst our family and friends, that my brothers Douglas and John were suffering terrible hardships due to broken marriages, and were trying to re-establish their lives in new relationships with new and existing children, and my sister Irene had great nervous and emotional difficulties arising from the menopause, and was, because of her independent nature, fighting to keep going in her own way, and hiding the signs of her distress. This was mostly unknown to her own caring family, but well known to Mom and me. All these, I realise, are common problems to many families throughout the world, but Mom was always sick with worry for her children. Her own difficulties she could handle, but her children's problems always devastated her. To her, the compensation money was enough to pay off her children's debts and give them a fresh chance. She was saying to me that at a spiritual level, she had arranged the sacrifice of her health for the compensation of the peace of knowing that she had given us all a fresh start.

I believe this is the exact truth, as I had, as I say, suspected it, but would not have voiced it, as to the average person it would sound so unbelievable. To those who can accept this, it is the bravest sacrifice imaginable. How the sequence of events leading to the accident could be arranged or even acceptable within God's Laws I do not know, but I do know there are far more things twixt heaven and earth than meet the eye.

All the circumstances surrounding the accident indicate that she was, in fact, the innocent victim, materially. It is far more likely that when she was in spirit, she assessed the situation and took advantage of it, knowing that the body which she had been so violently shaken out of was still usable. But, the courage to step back into all that pain is something else,. Mom had expressed the greatest gifts given by God - Love and Free will. She has also proved to me one of Christ's teachings, "As a tree falls, so shall it lie." meaning that the transition which we call death does not change our thoughts or intentions. Whatever we think before the transition, we carry on thinking immediately afterwards, be it good or bad. We are not instantly changed into an angel, or a devil for that matter, but how very frustrating for someone with very intense material desires to not have a material body through which to express them.

Just over a year after the accident, Mom's life had established a pattern and she became stable and contented. My wife Beryl or my sister Irene or sometimes both, would tend my Mom's needs every morning, then most days I would nip from work and run Mom and Irene to the pub at lunch time. There she would have a happy couple of hours with her friends and someone would usually run her home. In the evenings, my brothers or myself would visit her for an hour and then she would watch television with a tot of whisky and off to bed.

It was August '86 when my sister Irene came back from a holiday quite ill. She was taken into hospital and died the following morning. Mom was absolutely devastated, as indeed we all were. We knew she had problems, but this was totally unexpected even to her own doctor, who had suspected that she was suffering a nervous breakdown. To Mom it wasn't just the loss of her daughter, it was her companion, her best pal. It tore me apart to see her intense grief. Like the little trooper that she was though, she pulled herself together and carried on with her newly established pattern of life without her right hand.

No matter how off-colour Irene had felt, she had always turned up to look after Mom when it was her turn. Now Beryl took over, she had already nursed her father and mother right to the end of their lives and so was no stranger to caring. Although Mom was going through all the motions of continuing with the life she had fought so hard for, there was a strange emptiness in her eyes.

One evening after she had sat for healing she said, "Edwin, it is time that I went. Now that I have lost my lovely Irene there is nothing here for me. I have achieved that which I came back for and am quite contented in my soul. Thank you for helping me love, we have learned a lot together haven't we?" I just nodded and wept quietly for I knew that she was expressing free will and nothing on earth could change it this time. There was no further mention of this decision and had Mom not said anything, I would not have known. She carried on going out and fighting to improve her walking and laughed and enjoyed life. As Beryl cared for her and cleaned her flat and helped her to shower, a good relationship built up and they had many a good laugh together.

The Secret of Life

In November '86, the real decline began. She could no longer keep her food down and began to waste away. I was, fortunately, able to finish work for a while and between us we maintained Mom's comfort and dignity as best we could. In early January '87, she was in such intense pain and discomfort that she had to be admitted to St Luke's Hospice in Sheffield. It was heartbreaking to see the brilliant spark of her mind dulled by the effect of pain killing drugs. A spark which no amount of pain or hardship had managed to dim. On the 8th January I had the phone call which I was dreading, asking me to go and see her as she didn't have long left. It was a beautiful day for January and as I drove there, a huge orange sun hung low in the sky. When I arrived, she had just passed over and I went into the room alone to see her.

She lay there on her side with her eyes wide open looking out through the glass doors across the lawns and over the trees towards that huge orange sun. Her face, which looked fuller now, was glowing a healthy red and her eyes sparkled in the sunlight. There was a little smile on her lips. This was her body as she left it and this beautiful sight was the last she saw of earth. God could not have arranged it more perfectly. I wept just a short time, more conscious of my own loss, but happy for Mom. Knowing that she would still be standing nearby, I talked to her for a while and asked her to travel on with an easy mind, and promised to take care of everything and everyone just as we had arranged. I then prayed to God to receive her and that the guides may help her in any way necessary.

The cremation was the following week and as far as I was concerned, was merely a formality, - the disposing of that tiny shell which had served her so well. At the point in the service where the coffin passes through the curtains, I looked up from my prayers, because I had been to many funerals with Mom over the years and even with her knowledge of life and death, she had a strange phobia relating to that moment when the coffin disappears from view and usually would not look. As I looked, there she was, just beyond the minister as he prayed and just beyond the coffin as it slid slowly through the curtains.

She was sitting elegantly upon a tall wrought iron stool with her left leg crossed over her right. She was wearing a bright red overcoat with full three quarter sleeves and a black fur collar. On her head was a close fitting hat, nineteen twenties style, made of black shiny feathers. On her feet she wore very modern black suede bootees with soft wrinkled tops and very high heels. She looked like a forty year old model. She sat there with a perky little smile on her beautiful face, looking intently at me. When she registered that I had seen her, she looked back towards the coffin again. On her right hand was a black velvet glove and she held the left glove in that same hand. With a cocky little underhand swing of the loose glove, she ushered the coffin on its way, then turned back to smile at me and slowly faded away.

I have noticed over the years that whenever entities show themselves in this way, they always wear clothes which I could not have imagined and often make unexpected gestures, to make me realise, I think, that it is not my desire which created the image. Mom certainly had no phobia about her own cremation. Rather strangely, Mom has very rarely contacted me since that day. I had always imagined that being such a free traveller between the two worlds, she would frequently drop in for a chat. I think that she knows that her work on earth is finished and it is time for us all to stand alone.

Now and again, midst the embers of life,
there comes a tiny spark, blown by the
winds of the soul.
It burns with such intensity, that it
lends fire to all that it touches and
gives light to the whole world. .
Little Jenny was such a spark.
　　　　　　　　ER.

Chapter 5

My Sister Irene

Irene, mom and yours truly in October 1983, at my daughter Sonja's wedding reception slightly pie eyed and not knowing what the next three years were to bring and I thank God for that.

My Sister Irene

This is Irene aged 14 in less fiery mood. Probably free from the teasing of her wretch of a brother for a short time. She is sitting where I landed when she knocked me out of the yard and down the rockery.

When I think back to childhood with Irene, it is hard to realise the strong bond of love which linked us together. Irene was three years older than me and when she had passed the stage of protecting her little brother, she realised that as he grew up, he was turning into a mischievous and teasing little wretch who soon fired her flaming temper. By the time I was about ten, things between us were reaching fever pitch and I saw Irene as a target for my constant pranks.

Amongst her friends, Irene was known as the windmill, she was only small, but one wrong word from anyone, especially boys twice her size, and she would wade in with fists flailing sending them fleeing in terror. Consequently I stood little chance against her and remember many instances of being beaten up for my misdemeanour, the most vivid of which was when, after constant teasing, she retaliated by punching me straight on the nose, knocking me backwards over a little wall into a fence which collapsed, falling six feet into the garden with me on top of it. Whether the humiliation was greater than the pain I do not know, but I left her alone for a long time afterwards. Our constant squabbling, which upset our Mom terribly, came to a head when I was about thirteen and what started out to be a good hiding for me, turned into a fight which Irene lost, coming out of it with a terrible nose-bleed. The worm had turned. Afterwards I felt great remorse for having hurt her and realised how much I loved her. The feud was over.

Since that day, she confided many of her secrets and worries to me and we became the best of pals. I speak of these things to give some impression of the fire within her which affected the way in which she handled all things in her life. In contrast to this fire was a deep compassion for any person or animal who was weak or suffering. She had a son and two daughters and usually went out to work to help make ends meet, but still she found time to befriend and look after several old people, eventually looking after our mother when she needed her.

Irene became very interested in my spiritual experiences and unknown to me at the time, sought some of her own through the Ouija board. It all come to light when she sought my help after a terrifying experience. I believe that she sat with her eldest daughter and some friends for the session with the ouija board. They were successful in getting contacts as more often than not is the case when young women sit for such pursuits, The entities they attracted were, to say the least, questionable.

At that time, Irene worked mornings and was in the habit of meeting Mom in the pub at lunch time, then having an hour in bed in the afternoon to make up for her early start to the day. On the day in question, her younger daughter was off school with a slight illness and went to bed with her Mom for an hour. Irene was woken with a violent start, in the grip of a very powerful entity which she could not see, but could feel as it attacked her. She screamed and fought like a demon, meanwhile, her younger daughter, who I believe was only about six years old then, was shouting that a hand had got hold of her. Whilst Irene struggled, our mother who lived about half a mile away, had set off to walk to Irene's house, motivated by a strong feeling that something was very wrong. This was some time before she was hit by the car so she was able to cover the distance fairly quickly.

When Mom arrived at Irene's house, rather strangely she found that the back door was unlocked. She entered and went to the foot of the stairs. She shouted upstairs, "Are you all right Irene?" At the sound of Mom's voice the entity left Irene, who was quite shaken and still terrified. Irene was in no doubt at all about the identity of the entity, for he had spelt out his name on the Ouija board some days earlier and was someone she had known slightly, before his sudden death some months before. After the attack she was a little bruised and shaken. Her daughter, with childish innocence, described clearly the man whose hand held her and remembers the incident to this day.

During the nights that followed there were many little incidents indicating an unwelcome visitor in the house - a picture fell from the wall, doors opened on their own and the boards creaked all night. Both her daughters were terrified and unable to sleep and complained, either rightly or wrongly, of a presence as they lay in bed. Irene asked me if I could exorcise the house to get rid of her unwelcome visitor.

The first thing I did was to exercise my jaw and give her a thorough telling off for dabbling, in spite of warnings which I had given her, Her answer was to come out with the classical reply which I have heard so many times - "Well, I didn't think that it would hurt. It was only a bit of fun." Some fun! A serious problem had been created which could only be remedied by intense prayer and the help of my guides.

Some years before this incident, I had discussed exorcism with Mrs Lawton an old medium friend of mine and found that her physical remedy, coupled with prayer seemed to work very well. Maybe there is a need to visibly act in a way to satisfy the ego of the possessed person. I prefer to think that her remedy bears some weight. Normally, walking about waving canisters filled with burning incense and making loud chants and moans and such like perhaps appeals to people on this side, but I cannot see spirit taking any notice. The essence of what Mrs Lawton told me seemed to make sense so I adopted the method. She said, "Put a small amount of water into a glass and dissolve about a quarter of a teaspoon of salt into it. When you intercede for the person in trouble, hold your hands over the water and ask that God will bless it with a purity and high vibration, close to which no lower entity will wish to be. Dipping your fingers in the water, pass through all parts of the house sprinkling the water in every room. When the water evaporates, the salt will remain, still holding the essence of that high vibration and discouraging the mischievous spirit." Using this method certainly gives the body something to do and I find that it helps to intensify the prayer which is the real solution.

I called at Irene's house in the evening when my brother-in-law was out. He had stated clearly that had sensed nothing and quite rightly didn't really want to be involved with such affairs. The downstairs rooms were the first to be dealt with and I prayed through God within my mind as I went, asking for the guides to lead the disturbed one away and to heal him of his obsession.

When I went upstairs, I left the lights off so that I could get a better feel of the place. I entered the younger daughter's bedroom first and felt a distinct presence, the hairs on my neck stood up and I became icy cold. My first reaction was retaliation and scorn, I said, within my mind, "You cannot touch me, I am of God and of love," and as I said this, I was filled with a great power sizzling from head to foot. The scorn and challenge within me melted away and I felt only compassion for the disturbed one. I said, "Please let go of these things of the Earth and seek God in truth and in spirit. My guides are closing in to help you, please trust them and let them guide you towards the light where all will be clarified. Our love goes with you." At this, a great calm and emptiness settled over the house. I treated the other rooms, still praying as I went, but the work was already done.

When I went downstairs, Irene met me in the hall, she said, "He has gone, hasn't he? I felt him leave when you were in the back bedroom." I said, "Yes. Please don't bear a grudge, pray for him and it will clear your mind." The weeks which followed proved that the trouble was over and peace settled on the house again.

Irene was fortunate indeed, that the entity let go so easily. Even Christ's disciples had trouble with certain entities when they failed to free a man of a spirit which rendered him deaf and dumb, and Christ explained to them, "This kind can come forth by nothing, but by prayer and fasting."

When Irene entered the menopause, she began to suffer great stress just from the everyday problems of life. She sat for healing two or three times and although she admitted to feeling better afterwards, preferred to handle stress in her own way, by going out for a drink with Mom. She also began to smoke quite heavily and developed quite a nasty cough.

I was with Mom one Saturday morning when Irene came in, fresh from a holiday at the seaside. The first thing which I noticed was how brown she was and said, "Crikey! You've had some sun. It's been quite dull here." She said, "Well actually, I have hardly been out of the caravan all week as I have been suffering from a tummy bug." After a few minutes, I realised that she was not at all well and suggested that she should be at home in bed. She replied, "But I have come to see Mom and take her for a drink at dinner time." To cut a long story short, Mom and I eventually convinced her and I ran her home in the car. I then went back and gave Mom a lift to the pub where she could have a chat and a laugh with all her friends. Now the arrangement was that I would pick her up in an hour and a half and drop her off home. When I went to pick her up, I had my son, Dale, and his pal plus a lot of equipment in the car and a trailer on the back with three motor cycles on it as we were all off for an afternoon trials riding in the wilds.

When I walked into the pub, I was very surprised and a little annoyed to see Irene sitting there with Mom. She had walked the two hundred yards or so from her home to join Mom. I told her that she was extremely foolish and that she should be at home in bed. As Mom left with me, Irene stood up and said, "I think that I will go now, you can drop me off on the way." I said, "I can't possibly get you in the car Irene, we are so loaded up, there's only just enough room for Mom." Still a little annoyed at her irresponsible behaviour, I added rather nastily, "Besides, you managed to walk here, I am sure that you can make it back now that you have quenched your thirst." A young chap sitting nearby said, "It's all right Irene, I will walk you back if you don't feel very well." We left it at that and I dropped Mom off and enjoyed an afternoon out on the motorcycles with the lads.

On Monday morning, my wife Beryl called on the way back from Mom's flat to see how Irene was. When she came home she was very worried and said, "The doctor has been and says that Irene is suffering a nervous breakdown and has to go into hospital. They are waiting for the ambulance now. This morning she said that there was writing on the carpet and was reading long and eloquent passages from it, using words she could not have known. She was also pointing to what she said were bodies lying about the floor." I was extremely worried and very remorseful about my harsh words and actions towards her. Unfortunately, I always reacted this way to stress my annoyance at her determination to get on with life even at the expense of her health. When I phoned the hospital that evening, there came the standard reply, "She is as well as can be expected in the circumstances."

The following morning, I was in the bathroom, washing my hair, when the direct voice cut in loud and clear with the words, "Irene is dead." I was absolutely stunned and assumed this to be some trick of my imagination. The voice was so definite with that blunt statement that I found myself saying, "Please do not joke about such matters." When I went downstairs, Beryl said, "I am so worried about Irene." I told her about the direct voice and said, "Please don't worry, it may be some lesson I am being taught. I will phone the hospital as soon as I arrive at work.", but left home with a terrible dread in the pit of my stomach.

When I phoned the hospital, a doctor answered from the actual ward and said, "How close are you to Irene?" I replied, "I am her brother." He said, "But are you close to her?" "Of course I am," I replied. He said, "Just a moment," and went from the phone. A few moments later another male voice said, "Staff nurse here, are you close to your sister?" Again I replied, "Of course, I am her brother. Will you please tell me how she is?" There was a long pause and he replied, "She died at seven thirty this morning. I am most terribly sorry." "But what did she die of?" I asked. "It was pneumonia I'm afraid," he said. I didn't hear any more, it all fell into place. She wasn't having a nervous breakdown, she had been trying to get on with life whilst suffering from pneumonia and appeared brown because of jaundice due to collapsed liver.

How terrible she must have felt and still she had battled on, pretending that she was all right, not wanting to let people down, and me, of all people, had chastised her with my last words to her. How very often this happens when someone passes over. All that those who are close to them can remember saying were derogatory remarks. I have tried to comfort so many in this situation and now I have done the same! Her determination had fooled all the doctors, they completely missed the fact that she had pneumonia.

Mom! Oh dear God Mom! How am I going to break the news to her? I knew that she was having a check-up at the hospital that morning, I had to reach her before anyone else did. Making my apologies, I left work and went straight to the hospital. Mom had seen the consultant and was beginning the long wait for the ambulance to take her home. Up to this point, I had been far from tears and I knew that I must get her home to the comfort and seclusion of her flat before I told her. Walking up to her I said, "Hello Mom, I thought I would come and give you a lift home." Her face lit up and she said, "Oh Edwin, what a lovely surprise, it is awful waiting all that time for the ambulance." On the way back, I diverted the journey to take us past the old house which Mom had brought us up in for the bulk of our young lives and we reminisced on the way home. I made a pot of tea as soon as we arrived and she told me how pleased the doctors were with her miraculous progress since the accident. She could walk now with just one stick and her bowel cancer had not developed any more. Once again life was stable.

Kneeling by her chair, I took her hands and said, "Mom, I can hold back no longer. Irene died this morning." At first she did not believe me, but as she began to accept, I saw the spark of life dying in her eyes. It was then that we both broke down. I put my arms around her and we cried our cry, the rest of Mom's story I have already told. The tragic day was the fifth of August, 1986.

The following Monday was the day of the funeral. After a week of diminishing grief, by Sunday night, thoughts of the tragedy were like a distant memory and I went to bed with an easy mind. It was about five in the morning when I woke up with the by now familiar feeling of possession. I was lying on my right side and was totally paralysed, sizzling and unable to breathe. My eyes seemed to be open, and there, standing by the bed was Irene. She looked absolutely stunning in a powder blue two-piece costume, with a fitted skirt which came just to her knees, she wore matching powder blue high heeled shoes. Her hair was stylish and short, and although she had been fifty three when she passed, she looked about thirty five and bursting with life, energy and an air of controlled excitement. In her hand was a medium sized powder blue suitcase. My immediate reaction was one of delight at seeing her and I tried to physically say hello, fighting to free my mouth. As I did this, she started to fade, so realising my error, I relaxed back into the paralysis and she became solid and real again. Bending slightly, she put the suitcase down on the floor, then looked at me, registering my awareness of her. With an excited smile, she began to speak. She said, "Oh Edwin, I cannot begin to tell you how wonderful it all is. Everything is so marvellous." As she spoke, she bent down and opened the suitcase, putting something into it from her hand. Picking up the suitcase, she turned with a sense of controlled excitement and began to fade away, looking back at me with a little smile and a last wave as she disappeared through the fitted wardrobe. This was one of the most vivid and controlled manifestations which I have ever witnessed and left me in no doubt that everything was in order and lifted from my mind the awful guilt of my dreadful last words to her.

Later that day, after the funeral, as the family met for a cup of tea, I took Irene's husband, son and two daughters to one side and told them of the visit. Their grief turned to joy and to my surprise even her husband accepted what I said. They knew it was the truth. Instead of being left full of remorse at the tragic passing, they were delighted at the thought of Irene's joy and her new life. This is the way it should be.

A few weeks later, I met Irene again. In the early hours of the morning, I found myself in what at first I thought was a dream. [I realised that I was, in fact, in spirit, for during what transpired there was complete awareness of both the physical and spiritual state. The difference being, that in a dream one is usually only aware of the physical state.]

In the dream, I travelled to my mother's flat and as I entered through locked doors I thought to myself, "I am in the unifying body and am free for a while." As I went into the entrance hall of the flat complex, there, sitting at the bottom of the stairway, was Irene. She looked at me with some astonishment and said, "Edwin, what are you doing here? I didn't know that you could come into spirit." I laughed and said, "I told you that I had been coming here for years now, the question is what are you doing here? I thought you were still on holiday." She said, "I am waiting for Mom, she will be here soon and then we are going away together." I sat quietly by her on the stairs and we talked for what seemed to be an eternity about all that had happened in our lives. Eventually, the door to the corridor from Mom's flat opened and Mom walked through and took Irene's hand and turned to me saying, "I knew you wouldn't let me down. Peace of mind is God's greatest gift." I said, "Well, I come here quite often you know, it is a wonderful place, come and see." Turning, I walked through the doors into the street outside. Irene and Mom followed me, still holding hands and looking more like sisters than ever. The street was quite crowded with people, some going busily about their business, some just standing looking lost. I floated up into the air, stopping about thirty feet over the heads of the crowd. Irene and Mom looked up at me and I felt quite proud of being such an expert in astral travel. "Come on, it's quite easy," I shouted. Mom and Irene rose from the ground and soared effortlessly towards me, so, I began to ascend again, to lead the way. Suddenly I was stopped by a gentle resistance and could rise no further, and as I hovered there, fighting within my mind to travel on, Irene and Mom sailed effortlessly past me and as they disappeared into the sky, Mom shouted back, "It isn't your time yet Edwin." As I sank back to the ground and all the heavy people, I felt despondent and thought everything is so hard and so heavy here, and I can already feel the restriction of the bedclothes around me. Then I woke up thinking, "That truly was not a dream. I was in spirit."

The following day I went straight to Mom's flat and as I let myself in with my key, I realised that she was still in bed and I had a terrible dread that she had in fact passed over during the night, but she was quite all right. When I told her of the encounter with Irene, I avoided saying that she had come to take Mom with her, because at that point, Mom was just beginning to win her battle to rebuild her life without Irene. It was a week after this when she quietly told me that it was time for her to travel on, but I didn't say that Irene had already warned me, she probably knew.

End of Volume I

see page 66 for summary of Volume II

THE CROSS

One of my more predominant guides "Felicite De Lamennais" was a Jesuit Priest in the early eighteen hundreds and I write of him at some length in Chapter 17. Whenever he draws near to me in meditation, he impresses the image of the above cross upon my mind, to such an extent that I had the cross made in silver and wear it during healing. Even though I am well aware that healing is through prayer, not through material objects. With the realisation that I can only tend but a few of those in need of spiritual healing, I had cards printed with the image of the cross upon them.

I prayed over the cross and asked of God, that anyone in need of healing and asking through the focal point of it's image, may be tended by the hosts of healing guides who work through me.

With this intention, I show the cross above.

A number of people have contacted me over the years, to say that they have been helped after receiving the picture of the cross.

Some say that they simply held the cross to the disorder, or to their heart or head and said "please heal the condition dear God" and it was so.

I cannot accept credit for this, I am only the one who has accepted responsibility for small changes upon the earth plane. The healing guides are the givers, but by God's law, cannot intervene in our karmic state unless they are asked by someone on this side and only then if the soul in question has gleaned sufficient experience from the chosen disorder.

May God bless you and heal you.

Eddie

In the next three volumes "The Secret of Life" continues to unfold:

To help the uninitiated in their understanding of the remaining chapters, Volume II begins with descriptions of the following:

Chaper 6 - Types of Manifestation & Communication

Clairsentience - Clairvoyance - Clairaudience - Meditational - The Dream State - Trance - The Production of Ectoplasm - Automatic Writing - Psychic Art - Ouija Board - The Aura - The Unifying Body or Double - The Etheric Body - The Subtle Body - The Celestial Body or Shape of Light - Speaking in Tongues - Animals - Nature Spirits - The Lower Planes.

Chapter 7 - Dale

A Miracle of Visible Healing - Spirit Contact with Children -Spirit Help with Material Problems - Healing for Illness

Chapter 8 Sonja's Party -

Examples of Trance - The Production of Ectoplasm & Levitation - Irrational Fear of the Unknown - Personal Experience of the Production of Ectoplasm - A Demonstration of the use of Ectoplasmic Rods

Chapter 9 - Bob & Gertrude

The moving story of one couples fight for survival over illness and how spiritual healing prolonged their lives. Assisting someone through the transition called death. Incorporating the stories of some slightly unusual contacts with spirit

Chapter 10 - Rescue Work

The Young American - One of the most astonishing materialisations witnessed by the Author. That of a tragic young man searching desperately for help.
Beatty - A lady shocked by her own sudden transition to spirit, confused and frightened seeking explanations and wanting to tie up loose ends back on earth.

Chapter 11 Little Freddy

A kind and gentle soul who passed through life giving out love to all. He passed easily and sweetly into spirit and came back to take the Author out of his body and into spirit to Freddy's new spirit home, giving the Author an insight into that which we can inherit with a good and uncomplicated transition.
And so to Volume III

OTHER PUBLICATIONS BY CASDEC LTD

GHOST STATIONS SERIES
by BEST SELLING AUTHOR
Bruce Barrymore Halpenny

GHOST STATIONS 1 £5.99 The first book to bring you TRUE stories about the old abandoned airfields. The book has now reached cult status.

...In the still morning are the faint throb of a Lancaster Bomber could be clearly heard ... the dog ... runs to greet his Master. A light flickers from the derelict Control Tower and in the distance ... the sound of young men laughing and singing is carried on the wind as the mist rolls in across the deserted airfield ... these are the Ghost Squadrons.

GHOST STATIONS II £5.99 Sets the scene of those who wish to visit, whether on foot or, from the safety of their armchair ... the haunted airfields.

... In this volume you can read about the phantom aircraft and more about the Montrose Ghost ... the most famous ghost in the Royal Air Force. And weaving a sinister spell over deserted airfield ... the Keeper of Memories. The Lightning XS894 Mystery ... and the Harrier Jet mystery will give you food for thought.

GHOST STATIONS III £5.99 The truth about the 'Z' Men. Proof beyond any doubt that Glen Miller never died in December 1944 as the world was led to believe.

A spine chilling mystery ... Spirit of the Air Hero Ghost ... told in this volume for the first time. The truth about the Devil Dogs ... the hauntings of RAF Bentwaters ... Flying Saucers and Psychic Forces. And read why Borley Church is the most haunted church in the world. The Sentinel and the Ghost Squadrons ... Do the old airfields abound with Ghosts ...?

GHOST STATIONS IV £5.99 The concluding part of the Glen Miller Myth ... Was Miller a spy ...? Now told in THIS volume for the first time ... The Truth.

... The truth also about the Hess mystery ... the truth will shock you. The Loch Ness Ghost ... told for the first time in Ghost Stations IV. And official mythology exploded which could explain why the old airfield are haunted.

GHOST STATIONS V £5.99 Read about ... the phantom bed-checker of RAF Hereford ... Nigger - The mystery lives on ... the ghost squadrons of RAF Scampton ... the truth about the Lancester R5894 in Devil's Hill Field ... the ghosts of RAF Bawtry ... strange happenings in the South China Seas ... the Red Four mystery.

GHOST STATIONS VI £5.99 The lights were out in 1939 and 'Put that light out' was heard throughout this then green and pleasant land. A Christian Land. Bomber and Fighter airfields mushroomed overnight ... it was the spirit in these airfields and aircraft that fought to keep the world free. Many brave ... very brave, young men and women died.

GHOST STATIONS VII £5.99 Ghost Stations VII is brought out in December 1995 to meet the demands of Halpenny's readers who never seem to tire of his books on airfield ghosts, UFO's and mystery.

The Secret of Life

CASDEC HERITAGE SERIES

GHOST TRAILS OF NORTHUMBRIA £3.99 *by Clive Kristen* This trend-setting title remains as popular as ever. The ghost-hunter is invited to follow five trails that lead to some of the region's classic haunts. Award-winning pictures, maps, and a full historical glossary complement the lively and entertaining text.

MORE GHOST TRAILS OF NORTHUMBRIA £3.99 *by Clive Kristen* Following the spooktacular success of Ghost Trails of Northumbria it is not surprising that this second foray into the world of the supernatural became an instant best seller.

MURDER AND MYSTERY TRAILS OF NORTHUMBRIA £3.99 *by Clive Kristen* This companion volume to the Ghost Trails books develops the tour and explore the theme against a background of dubious departures, early exits and horrible happenings. Murder and Mystery Trails again features the award-winning team of photographer Duncan Elson, and illustrator Mark Nuttall.

A PEDALLER'S TALES £2.25 *by Chris Rooney* Popular postie, Chris Rooney leapt into the Casdec saddle with a book that has found favour with all those who enjoy classic countryside and the freedom of the road. So why not join Chris and his cast of colourful characters as they set off in search of adventure?

TASTY TRAILS OF NORTHUMBRIA £4.99 *by Jill Harrison* Northumbria has a culinary heritage that can be traced back more than 1000 years. Farmer's wife, Jill Harrison, has woven her account of the very best of Northumbria fare into the popular CASDEC trails format. If you enjoy the taste of tradition and all that is best today you will find FOOD TRAILS is the gourmet's delight. Wonderfully illustrated by Jill's Aunt.

GHOST TRAILS OF THE YORKSHIRE DALES £6.49 *by Clive Kristen* Following the success of the Ghost Trails of Northumbria series, author Clive Kristen invites you to explore the supernatural world of the delightful Yorkshire Dales.

CYCLING TRAILS OF THE YORKSHIRE DALES £5.49 *by David Johnson* Veteran cyclist David Johnson, helps you to enjoy the byeways of the Yorkshire Dales. Certain to become a favourite with cyclists of all ages, the book is packed with anecdotes and advice as well as the customary maps and pictures.

Village Trails of Northumbria £4.99 *by Andrew Waterhouse* Northumbria's villages are an Aladdin's cave of hidden delights for anyone interested in local history and the great outdoors. Join Andrew Waterhouse on his tours of some of the most attractive and fascinating villages in Britain.

OTHER TITLES

STUDIES IN SCARLET £4.95 *by John West* "The man's body was lying on the bedstead in a state of nudity, its left hand pressed to its heart and the right hand convulsively clutching the hair. And oppressive odour as of scorched fat prevailed the room. No wound was obvious upon the body but the chest was transversally barred in several places by dull red stripes. A deep and broad burn was exhibited in the middle of the back and the spine was found to be completely carbonised".

The horrific tale is just one of the many true life stories that form the basis of a fascinating and gruesome study into the darker side of Victorian society.